Fiction International 55

Fiction International is a journal of arts and culture published at San Diego State University. *Fiction International* was founded, published, and edited by Joe David Bellamy at St. Lawrence University from 1973 to 1982.

Business correspondence, including that related to subscriptions and advertising, should be directed to:

Harold Jaffe
Editor, *Fiction International*
Department of English
San Diego State University
5500 Campanile Drive
San Diego, CA 92182–6020

E-mail: fictioninternational@gmail.com

Cover: Giorgio de Chirico, *Mystery and Melancholy of a Street* (1914)

Typesetting & design by Norman Conquest

ISSN 0092-1912
ISBN 978-0-931362-20-0

Call for Submissions: Refugee

Fiction International is accepting submissions for: REFUGEE. Submissions will be accepted online or through mail from October 1, 2022 to February 15, 2023. Submissions may include fiction, non-fiction, visuals, and indeterminate texts reflecting the theme.

Online submissions must be submitted through Submittable at **fictioninternational.submittable.com/submit**

Hard copy submissions must be accompanied by a SASE, and mailed to:

Harold Jaffe
Editor, *Fiction International*
Department of English
San Diego State University
5500 Campanile Drive
San Diego, CA 92182–6020
Queries: hjaffe@sdsu.edu

We exercise all due care in handling manuscripts, but we cannot be responsible for loss. Please allow one to three months for reply. If submitting through Submittable or mail isn't possible, we may accept emailed submissions **providing you receive approval in advance**. Should you have any questions, please email the editor: **hjaffe@sdsu.edu**

Subscriptions

Fiction International is published once yearly. Annual subscriptions: Individuals: $16 plus $2 postage for U.S. / $16 plus $4 postage for international addresses. Institutions: If subscription is issued through a subscription service, their terms and rates apply. Otherwise, the rates are: $35 plus $2 postage for U.S. / $35 plus $4 postage for international addresses. Some past issues are also for sale. Please see our website (**fictioninternational.sdsu.edu**) for a complete list of available past issues and prices. Remember to add applicable postage when ordering.

Use of FI in the Classroom

Please consider assigning this issue (or one of the past issues) as part of your reading list. Ask your bookseller to contact Harold Jaffe (hjaffe@mail.sdsu.edu) for information on availability of multiple copies.

Donating to FI

Although we maintain an office at San Diego State University, *Fiction International* is 100% independent of financial aid from the university. Outside of sales and subscriptions, our continued existence relies on supporters who make cash donations. That is why we are asking people who support the artistic merit of the journal and the progressive political thinking it advances to support Fiction International by making a tax-deductible donation.If you would like to donate to Fiction International using a credit card, please visit our website (fictioninternational.sdsu.edu) and use the "Donate" button to link to our PayPal account. You may also mail a check to: *Fiction International,* Department of English, San Diego State University, 5500 Campanile Drive, San Diego, CA 92182-6020

Support FI Online

Fiction International maintains an active online presence through its website, Twitter, and Facebook. Please support us by visiting the following addresses and by recommending us to family and friends.

fictioninternational.sdsu.edu
twitter.com/FictIntl
facebook.com/FictIntl

Contents

7	**Nick Sweeney** Visual
9	**William Repass** The Proposal
14	**Elizabeth Brus** Tsepiso's Life, Recorded
17	**Arthur M. Doweyko** Visual
18	**Elaine Monaghan** An Unfortunate Accident
21	**Douglas Cole** Clypto
28	**Joel Lipman** Visual
29	**R. Bennett** Auricle / Ventricle
41	**Adam Peterson** The Grandmas Dream of Revolution
44	**Brandon Hansen** The Long Lake Dream
56	**Joel Lipman** Visual
57	**Nathan Alling Long** The Table and Everything on It
60	**Susan A. H. Grace** Girl with Chrysanthemums
73	**J. Condra Smith** Nork
82	**Marc Levy** Visual
83	**Toby Olson** Larosa Dreaming
88	**Michelle DeLong** Dreaming of J. Peterman
90	**Nancy J. Fagan** Love in the Time of Tumor
105	**Joel Lipman** Visual
106	**AE Reiff** Moo Cow
110	**Suzana Stojanović** Orange Tree
115	**James McNally** Brooklyn
117	**William Blake** Visual
118	**Stephen-Paul Martin** Song for Our Ancestors
138	**Robert James Cross** Emergence
147	**Robert L. Penick** Dream State
148	**Robert Boucheron** The Writer in the Tower
155	**Nick Sweeney** Magic Pictures - A Dream of the Eastern Roman Empire
159	**Joel Lipman** Visual
160	**Benjamin Abtan** The Third Child
172	**Sara Jacobson** Cotton Candy Hills
175	**Robert James Cross** Visual
176	**Mark DiFruscio** Land of the Heart's Desire
193	**Tom Whalen** Four Micro-Fictions
196	**Dmitry Borshch** Visual
197	**Quinn Adikes** Scoochie
210	**Joel Lipman** Visual
211	**David Luntz** The Secret History of Fritz Lang
214	**Quentin Bailey & Harold Jaffe** Dream Discourse
227	Contributor Notes

Nick Sweeney

William Repass

The Proposal

In response to *pervasive discontent* from service industry personnel, and after much deliberation, denunciation, and sectarian splintering, the Ahistorical Society (AS) and Autumn Unity (AU), alongside the newly formed Stateless State Faction (SSF) and Decadence / Disintegration Task Force (DTF), release for *public scrutiny* the following PROPOSAL: That the Gregorian Calendar, along with its accessory, clock-time, which have proven *woefully adequate* to the organization and coordination of social time, be dissolved. With an eye towards rapid desynchronization and autolysis of the social cadaver, we further propose the adoption of a *new temporal paradigm* (NTP) along the following parameters:

1. That all clocks be unplugged / allowed to run out of batteries, leaving countless localized reminders of the *obsolete and obscene* clock-time regime. Let such numerals as "5:35" shrug off the burden of meaning.

2. That all wall calendars, appointment books, and work schedules be deleted / erased / torn down, superseded by a cake or sandwich (submarine where feasible—SSF) procured from a corner grocery and placed under glass, plastic, or other translucent material.

§ That the disintegration of specified foodstuffs serve as the *social yardstick de jure* of time's convulsions.

3. That the clock-time "second," based on the photon absorption by transitions between the two hyperfine ground states of caesium-133 atoms, be scrapped in favor of the interval required for the *temporal subject* to undergo one twinge of anxiety regarding time's ephemeral "nature" in a mortality-based context.

§ That from this point forward, temporal subjects refer to such intervals as *throbs* (*tics* having been rejected as too suggestive of timeclock discipline).

4. That what is called a "dark spiral" of such forebodings supplant the clock-time "minute." This interval may *dilate* as temporal subjects, freed from the manacles of clock-time (AS), habituate to the new temporal paradigm. Should its *contraction* instead become the trend, in no way will this undermine said paradigm (DTF).

§ That from this point forward, temporal subjects refer to such intervals as *volutes* (AS, SSF) or *torques* (DTF, AU), their preference.

5. That the timeclock "hour" be usurped by the interval required for the temporal subject to grow bored of whatever (in)activity should happen to engage them at any given throb, such that the "10 minutes" of clock-time spent in tedium and felt as an "hour" no longer stand as a contradiction.

§ That from this point forward, temporal subjects refer to such intervals of unalienated continuity as *spells* (unanimous approval).

6. That the clock-time "24-hour day" be replaced with the interval between two *dreamtimes* (self-explanatory—AS), be they catnaps or marathons. Let waking life be severed from its archaic subordination to sunlight's Apollonianism, while the life of dreams sheds its stigma as "unproductive" and returns from exile in the shadows. Should temporal subjects prefer diurnal to nocturnal or semi-nocturnal rhythms, let them sleep at their discretion (AU).

§ That from this point forward, temporal subjects refer to such intervals as *awhiles* (AS, AU), *betweenities* (SSF) or *untils* (DTF).

§ That temporal subjects refer to intervals of sleep as *dreamtimes*, regardless of whether dreaming occurs, with emphasis on the achronology experienced in dreams, as opposed to its annihilation in dreamless sleep. [N.B., the SSF takes umbrage at the suggestion that dreamless sleep is experienced atemporally, tantamount to a *non-experience*. The term *temporal subject* would in this case lose all coherence, paradoxically decelerating autolysis].

7. That the Gregorian "week" be replaced by the interval of five dreamtimes, with one *workawhile*, *betweensleep*, or *workuntil* bookended by four dreamtimes. The minimum of work required for continual dysfunction of asynchronic society will transpire during this interposed awhile / betweenity / until for one or two spells to start with, say, until the distinction between work and play liquefies entirely.

§ That from this point forward, temporal subjects refer to such intervals as *severals* (passed with, ahem, several abstentions).

8. That the Gregorian "month" be fed to the *trash compactor of ahistory* and replaced with... nothing. Such an interval serves no dysfunction under NTP.

9. That the Gregorian "season" be similarly trashed, in favor of *waves* that correspond to the climate extremes already suffered during the "months" of this coalition's deliberation, denunciation, etc. [N.B. AU favors the adoption of one season, Autumn, more for the symbolic associations of melancholy, withering, and saudade, than for any empirical reason.]

§ That from this point forward, temporal subjects refer to such waves as *Siberian* and *Saharan*.

10. That the interval of one Gregorian "year" be replaced by one Siberian followed by one Saharan Wave, reflecting the trend towards Heat Death. Or, in the "unlikely event" (AS) of the adoption of AU's amendment to subproposal 9, that Autumn begin and end at the Saharan zenith / Siberian nadir.

11. That the Gregorian "century" be jettisoned and left unreplaced, as the coalition reached no consensus during the time allotted (in the "future," such allotments will be a condition of the "past") for deliberation, denunciation, etc., on the questions of whether asynchronic society would or should bother to sustain itself that long; whether asychronic society should be termed a "society" at all; whether the pseudo-Gregorian "generation" is too anthropocentric or not enough, let alone too stable or unstable an interval under the rapid autolysis of the social cadaver; whether some intermediate temporal category should be devised to account for that disintegrating sandwich

(or cake) placed under a bell jar in subproposal 2; whether the adoption of a new temporal regime by an organized body would not simply codify an already operative paradigm; whether the presumed authority of such a "body" (albeit splintered) is not an *affront to Entropy herself*; whether "Entropy" should be capitalized, anthropomorphized, gendered, struggled for in the name of, or named.

§ Be that as it may, by "then," when the Gregorian century is forgotten, when asynchronic society has lost the need for temporal paradigms, might fruiting bodies mushroom from fruitlessness?

12. Disorganize one sector of the universe and, like it or not, you organize another.

Elizabeth Brus

Tsepiso's Life, Recorded

In the valley below the Maloti Mountains of Lesotho, green fingers that hum with the sound of the sun, a mother gives birth. Cuban doctors smoke cigarettes at the hospital down the road, but the mother labors alone, ripping her flesh from one end to the other, blood spraying her yellow towels like a broken dam. The baby spends the first months of her life wrapped in a purple Disney towel with two princesses. When she bathes, she opens and closes her mouth like a fish and stretches her rope-like legs in the water of the metal bucket. The mother rubs her thumb on her baby's yellow forehead and whispers promises in her ear, casting her dreams beyond her own little life selling peaches by the side of the road. Sometimes, when the baby bites her nipple, or when the mother must smear medicine on the birthing cut under her skirt, she leaves the baby by the window until the baby stops crying. The baby listens to the noise of the moon and the men in the bar down the road.

On her first birthday, the mother names the baby Tsepiso. She has eyes with a touch of blue when the sun squints. Because she looks like them, the elderly French nuns in the clinic down the road dote on her, and give her red shoes from France. Not her father's eyes, the other women murmur as they weed their gardens, bent at the waist, lips pointed to the ground. The whisper reaches the coal mines where the father works in Gauteng, and the cheques in the blue envelopes, delivered every first Friday to the post office by the Chinese shop, arrive erratically, and then stop. After some months of phone calls and stiff-necked walks by the women at the village pump, Tsepiso's mother sells the family's two sheep, and swaps her favorite Tlotsa lotion from the Shop Rite for the free glycerin tubes from the clinic.

Tsepiso runs up and down the dirt road with her red shoes until she trips and falls on a rock, ripping the flesh on her cheek. She throws her red shoes in the latrine by the empty sheep pen and watches them sink into the family shit, her face flushed and wet with tears and a crescent of blood. Her mother beats her for the first time in her life, clumsy and hesitant, because she cannot buy her new shoes without the blue cheques.

When Tsepiso turns seven, the nuns agree to pay 400 rand for her primary school fees in exchange for her work in the clinic. The clinic is quiet, and Tsepiso has time to teach herself reading and fractions. Tsepiso sits behind a grand mahogany desk with engravings on the leg joints and hands out tablets to women from the village who line up outside. They resent going to the white nuns for their medicine, and set their faces like the hills that ring the village, melodic and indifferent. Sometimes, the nuns hand out square-wrapped rubber circles and special tablets to girls who linger by the kitchen door at dusk. One day, the priest visits, and the nuns hide the square-wrapped rubber circles and special tablets in the linen closet. When Tsepiso tells her mother about the priest's visit, her mother beats her for the second time in her life, because she cannot protect her daughter from the choices of men. Tsepiso squats in the corn fields behind her house, rubbing her sore palms, her thoughts black and scattered with the knowledge that nuns can lie.

When Tsepiso turns twelve, her friends advise her to find a mohlankana to build a life outside the village, so she befriends a man at the local bar. Soon, he meets her behind the school washroom at night, and she puts sand inside her to increase his pleasure. After, in private, she examines the tiny tears in her flesh and pictures them like the little rivers that drip from the top of the mountains. She hides the money he gives her in a tin in the clinic.

Tsepiso's studies improve, and she passes at the top of her class. Out of her 312 classmates, Tsepiso's teachers choose her for the high school scholarship, and she runs home with the paper that shows her mother that she will only have to pay 4,050 rand, or 15% of the expected tuition. Her mother puts down the wild moroho she has gathered for dinner, puts down the salt, and looks at the white paper. She studies her daughter's almost-blue eyes, rubs her thumb on the scar on her cheek, and tells her that in a month she will go to Gauteng, 600 km away, to work as a housekeeper.

The next day, Tsepiso fetches the scholarship paper and the tin from the clinic to count her money. She needs only 270 rand, and goes to the bar by the school to wait for the man. She squats in the heat by the tree, but when he sees her, his face folds on itself like the mountains, and he turns away.

After some time, she walks to the river to the west of the village, a place she's never been, and sits with her feet in the water, her face turned to the velvet facade of moss and rock above her. The sun sings, high and low.

At nightfall, she returns with the tin of money, and her mother beats her for the third and final time in her life, but for the first time in anger, her cheeks red like her daughter's back.

In the fall, Tsepiso packs a bag with a new pair of shoes from her mother and climbs into a crowded taxi, her knees pressed to her chest to make room for others. A year later, with a baby twisted the wrong way inside of her, she dies, in a shack down the highway from a silver skyscraper, her thoughts clanging with the sound of the sun and slipping out of sight behind the tops of the velvet mountains.

Arthur M. Doweyko

Elaine Monaghan

An Unfortunate Accident

Helen is looking down at me sympathetically and it's an unfamiliar feeling. She is wordlessly twisting her long, golden hair into a perfect knot. At the same time, I know she is fighting not to purse her heart-shaped, fleshy mouth at the blood gushing from my torn-up foot. I look up at her to see if the sympathy lasts more than a split second but the sun has made a halo behind her head and I am blinded.

"You're late," I say, and hesitate. You know how it is, when you have a friend who is more beautiful, more connected, and you need them and you're terrified to lose them? But the gaping mouth that has opened up in the upper side of my big toe is throbbing and I've already bled through all my tissues trying to hold the edges together so it doesn't seem like such a gamble to finish the thought. "As usual."

I still can't see Helen's face and she still has nothing to say but I can hear her astonishment. She sighs that little, melodic sigh, the one I imagine she occasionally evinced while lifting her leg higher than all the other gymnasts back home in New York even though she never, ever practiced. "I think there's a Klinik over on the corner of Katzbachstrasse," she says, showing off again with that perfectly clipped accent she no doubt uses to dramatic effect in the Gymnasium where, like me, she is teaching English to leering high-school boys. I mean, is it really necessary to pronounce all the names of German streets in an authentically German accent when you're speaking English to an English speaker? "I think you're going to need stitches."

Because she was late, and the sun was hot, and the blades of grass in Viktoriapark had grown lush with the April rains, and my feet were hopelessly sweaty, I had kicked off my socks and shoes. It seemed like such a minor expression of abandon compared to the rows upon rows of Berliners who had stripped naked because it was the May Day holiday, though they never needed an excuse. Lines and lines of them as far as the eye could see, up and down the hills by the score, rolling over from time to time so that hundreds of pale phalluses would suddenly come into view like they were the entire flute section of a gigantic orchestra picking up the refrain and absolutely demanding our attention. So, in an attempt to distract myself, really, I had run through the grass, showing the world what an excellent time I was having, by myself, even though my gorgeous friend was late as usual, until my left foot found itself kicking a broken beer glass someone had left behind. It flew several feet and landed gently in the grass.

I sat down to examine my foot. The wounds hurt like crazy and quickly began to throb, and for a few seconds the situation seemed manageable. But then blood started to flow from the biggest opening on the upper side of my toe. The gash ran from the outer corner of the nail diagonally across the toe and extended into a spiral-shaped opening between my big and my second toes and then continued for some indeterminable length under my foot. The blood was flowing into the grass now, droplets at first like dew, then like scarlet puddles, and so I grabbed tissues from my bag and tried to tie the biggest hole together. But the little mouth just wouldn't stay closed. It kept its little self open, a newborn baby screaming.

I look up again at Helen but now she is just a silhouette against a blazing backdrop, her voice like molasses. "I really think we need to go to the Klinik." She continues to say words that sound like a recording that has been slowed almost to a standstill, distorted to the point of incomprehensibility. I try to say words too, but nothing comes out. Only the mouth in my foot is speaking.

Now I am falling, flying through the grass and into the bowels of Berlin, and find myself in an underground train. I am with Helen, and I am holding a baby that is wrapped in swaddling cloth except it looks like bandages. It is tiny, too tiny to be breathing by itself, certainly too tiny to be looking at me with that sly smile. Helen is twisting her hair and making eyes at some guy who is playing the guitar and singing, lips like Mick Jagger. She is smiling and he is leering and I think I'm going to be sick.

The train stops suddenly and I bang my head on the window. I get out the train and find myself in a dark corridor. It is daytime but the corridor is so dim I can barely make out the wallpaper, which is midnight blue and feels like velour to the touch. Helen is gone now. At the end of a corridor is a door with frosted glass. I hear a gentle drumbeat of quiet murmurings, women's murmurings. I know I have to go there but I don't want to go.

To my right, Alex appears. His hands are thrust deep into his jean pockets, and he's wearing the worker's hat and leather jacket he stole right before he moved out my apartment, not long after the rape. "You don't need to go in," he is saying with the evil sneer that I once mistook for cultural differences when in actuality he wanted to kill me. "I'll look after you. You can come and live with my family."

I open my mouth in a silent scream and keep walking towards the frosted door. It opens and a nurse ushers me in. I can feel Alex's breath on the back of my neck, and he is treading on my shoe where it meets my right ankle as I quickly shut and lock the door behind me.

"How many weeks?" the woman in the next bed is asking me. "Twelve," I say.

"What do you do with the remains?" I ask the doctor, but he is putting a muzzle on my mouth and I am falling asleep.

I wake up, this time in a bus, and we are passing lambs gamboling in lush green fields. It is lambing season, and I hear the sheep bleat. I am alone in the back row. No one is disturbing us. I look down and realize I am holding a tiny baby the size of my big toe in my hand. It is looking at me and smiling.

Its mouth opens. "It's okay," it says. "You'll be okay. I love you."

Douglas Cole

Clypto

I won't tell you the title or the author's name. Why take the risk? I wouldn't intentionally inflict that on anyone. Not intentionally. We had signed the papers, completing the refinance—taking advantage of that low interest, and I'm not sentimental, but staring down the thirty years of that new mortgage, that end-date—well, I can tell you it crossed my mind that I might not make it that far. Who's got thirty years guaranteed? But you do the sensible thing. You follow the trends. Herd immunity. There is something very comfortable and safe about anonymity.

Without even thinking about it, I pulled my feet back before the sunlight could even touch me. Do you remember those games you used to play as a kid where the floor is made out of acid and you have to jump around on the furniture to stay alive? I was in something of a spot like that. You see, this book I was reading was one of these big books, more than five hundred pages. The kind of thing where you sort of forget things as you go, but the smart writer gives you little hints, little reminders. I was pretty deep into it by this point. I was committed. Certain details did stand out—the main character slept a lot. In fact, it seemed like a lot of attention was spent on eating and sleeping. I even thought at one point, is this going anywhere? But some books are just like relationships—you stick with them: till death do us part.

Look, I've got to get this one thing out of the way. I've lost myself in a good book before. Sometimes it's like I dissolve right out of the world and—see, this one time I was reading, and I was reading one of those sort of scary, horror novels, house built on an ancient burial ground sort of thing, and it's late, just one light on over my shoulder and—bam! A light goes on at the other end of the couch. Lights go off all the time, right? But on? That's different. I switched it off. Bam! It goes on again. I don't know what you would do, but I stopped reading then and there. I didn't finish that book until daylight.

There's not much else to that story. I'm not the superstitious type, okay? That's the point. So when I tell you I was reading this big book and this character spends a lot of time on the couch, cleaning the kitchen, wandering around the neighborhood—did I mention he was out of work? I was too, but that's hardly a coincidence. At this point, lots of people are. I wasn't seeing a lot of parallels. No lights were going on in the room. But, and this is where things get a little weird—I have this chair. It's just a normal chair, like a dining chair with a high back and a sort of maroon-colored fabric on the seat. Now that's what I remember? I'm very clear on this. So, when I see not my old boring dining chair but a slick, black-leather arm chair, the kind of thing you'd find in a nice office—see, there's a moment when it's not even a shock. Sure, I'd thought of getting one like that. I think I might have looked at a few of them in office stores, even sat in a few and thought, wow, there is a difference between the one for two hundred and the one for five hundred. I usually think that kind of thing is a scam. You wouldn't think it would make that much of a difference—the way it feels, the plushness, the way it springs back after leaning back in it—but the thing is, I didn't buy that chair. I have no memory of bringing it home. But I do have this distinct memory of reading about a chair like that in this book!

I know what extended time off can do to the mind. So, I'm on the alert. I can tell the signs, so I went back looking for the description of the chair in that book. I had to be sure of this. I mean, I know I saw it. But have you ever gone searching for a passage, a phrase in a book, a big book especially, and you know it's there but god help you it's literally like looking for a needle in a haystack? I don't know how many hours I was at it before I realized I'd have to start at the beginning and read forward from there, and I wasn't going to do that. But you can believe me when I tell you I was marking that text judiciously after that! Anything I thought significant I underlined. I made notes and cross-referenced. Nothing too small was going to escape my attention. If something was going to pop up here in the real world out of that book, I would know where it came from.

And I liked the chair. I admit I couldn't sit in it at first. I thought if I did I might find myself hurtling warp-speed into another reality. I know the thought was ridiculous, but haven't you ever chosen a conservative course even if it seems a bit paranoid? Though, why take a chance? Now, nothing else suddenly appeared like that chair. But it's almost like a virus mutating to get around the immune system, to think of an analogy. No. But what did happen was a delivery. A big package shows up on the porch, an identical set of garden trellises. Had I thought of getting one of those? Maybe. Certainly not two. Could I use them? When we first moved into this place, there was an iron railing that cut the front yard in half. It was there because the previous owner had big dogs. I'm speculating here, but I'm quite sure. I tried digging it out, but can you believe it, it was attached to a cement wall underground. I know, I dug down so far I found myself standing in a hole so deep the surface was over my head. This is dangerous, I thought. And I don't know what I was planning to do with that wall anyway—jackhammer the cement? I've used a jackhammer before! I just filled the hole back up and cut the fence off at the base with a hacksaw. I thought, that was quite ingenious. Who will know there is a wall underground? But there was a morning glory vine that had pretty well established a perch on that railing. And my partner fell in love with that plant. This is something I can understand. So I didn't cut it out. I did some damage pulling it off the fence, and it got pretty sad and droopy without something to hold onto. I promised my partner I'd find something else for it to climb on, but you know how promises go— the best intentions and all. And here again, I swear there was some mention of a garden trellis in that book. Hand to heart. But search as I might, I could not find the reference.

Okay, it did occur to me that this might be some strange and mystical book in which every detail it throws out into the word—chair, trellis—vanishes from its pages.

There's a certain logic in that, don't you think? And I should also mention that it was a translation. That's right. It was written in another language and then translated. So, were already into things being once or more removed. That might be an important factor. I don't know. But it is contemporary book. Once again, no, I'm not going to tell you the title of the book or the name of the author. I'm not that irresponsible.

So I made use of the chair. It's a comfortable chair. And I set up the trellises. It's good to keep a promise, after all. And the second one, you wonder? Well, I used it for the Dame Rocket I discovered one summer evening on a walk with my dog, The Dude. It called out to me by scent, a distress signal it turns out. That's how it communicates. I knelt down beside it and there it was, crushed, it seemed, by someone backing over it. It wasn't until I got it home and saw the bright green paint mark on it—meaning it was marked for death. The city does this in certain areas for certain plants. Turns out not everyone loves the Dame Rocket. Some even consider it a noxious, invasive weed. I didn't think it was going to make it, but after I put it in a bucket of water, it perked up, so I planted it under the Buddha fountain. It's got the heart of a lion, that Dame Rocket. And it does like to spread out. So I gave it a trellis. What culture is it that says when you save someone's life you're responsible for it forever?

So then other things appeared—not by mail, but maybe a stencil shows up in the garage with the words "Wild Blue Yonder." That was a weird one, because I think, and I could be wrong because this book has a lot of chapters (I kind of like it when a writer breaks up a book into a lot of chapters so that you read each one in a sitting and get a chance to just absorb it), but I think there was a chapter called "The Wild Blue Yonder." You can be very sure of a thing, and then…. It wasn't in my index. I'd started a separate set of note cards with recurring images and ideas catalogued on them—nothing was going to get past my censor. I went back through the pages. I searched and searched. I know it must be in here somewhere, but you can't mark everything. Then it's like not marking anything at all. I couldn't find "Wild Blue Yonder." I threw my hands up. I give up! But it's a fun thing to paint on the back fence gate, you know? You leave your little garden and head out into…

It was getting a little unsettling, though, to keep on reading. The malaise of the character's days seemed to bleed over in the drift of clouds over my peninsula, the routine walks with the dog, the eating, the cleaning, the sleeping. There was a not a lot to distinguish between the two of us. I had to look up what day of the week it was. At one point another character tells the main character about his time in the war, the trauma of it and how after he returns home he never feels love, never marries, never connects with anyone. He feels like an empty shell. That's pretty specific. So how do you think I reacted when my neighbor across the alleyway, who never talks to anyone and who sits at night by a fire pit in his back yard alone, one afternoon when he sees me bringing in the garbage cans from the alleyway at the same time he's bringing in his says to me "It's like my time in the military…marching in step."

The book took on a haunting glow. I would only read a few pages a day. Either way, it's a problem, now. I read, and what's inside weaves into my dreams. And here's the real kicker—sometimes I come upon a moment in the book that looks a lot like something I've seen before, not in the book but out here. What do you do in a case like this? And if I don't keep reading, I think, who knows what fate-lines I'll trip over. I mean, a promise is a promise. I did long ago decide that if I didn't like a book I was reading I would stop. There's always something better out there, and life is short, so why stick with something I'm not enjoying? But this one's got a hook in me. So how do you expect me to react when I come upon a passage like this: "I felt as if I had become a part of a badly written novel, that someone was taking me to task for being utterly unreal." Well, I can tell you, when I read that my heart about stopped. I mean, who's in charge here? I might have too much time on my hands, too much space. The edges are getting a little fuzzy.

"Why don't you stop reading it?" my partner said.

"I don't know. I'm both repulsed and curious."

"Well, then I can't help you."

"Was I asking for help?"

"You seem distressed."

"I do?" I thought I was outwardly calm. My heartrate seemed relatively slow. But I did indeed keep on reading.

It got so chaotic that at one point I was making an annotation, writing on a blank page at the back of the book a little note about something I'd read, one of the recurring images that I would include on a notecard—water, I think, and I could have sworn I'd already done this. I could remember doing this maybe a year ago, way before I started reading the book. The pages, the notes I was making, the thought I was having—does this go into this category or that one?—a loop. I was obviously stuck in a loop. But something was daily, weekly, (who knows how often), erasing my memory of it.

Strange as it was these things were popping up in my reality, perhaps most odd and more disturbing was the voice. It called itself Crypto or Clypto. I think Clypto. It didn't say "I am Clypto," but it sent it like a text written on the inside of my eyelids—just that—Clypto. But it was like a banner, an announcement, or maybe an introduction, I don't know the intent, or maybe it was more like a signature, the kind of thing you see in the lower corner of a painting: the artist known as Clypto. Which itself was just the kind of thing I might write off as my own imagination, a bit of dream fluff, if I hadn't seen it after that graffiti scripted on a water tank at the top of the hill and later on a boxcar and then on a wall of a building near to being demolished and then the span of an overpass—Clypto. Sometimes it looked like Clepto. Sometimes is looked like Crypto, in that hyper-stylized lettering of super-silver and neon green, overlapping and curling like cartoon characters coming out of the screen.

So I went back to the book, looking for Clypto. I hadn't seen it before, but now I was expecting it to show up any minute. I couldn't be sure which direction this current was flowing. And this is where things got a little more concerning because at about this point in the book the main character's wife goes missing. You know how this sort of thing goes if you've ever read any mystery or crime stories or watched any of those documentaries or movies—the husband is always the prime suspect. You can see where this is going, right? I'm not waiting around for the other shoe to drop. I'm getting proactive.

And that's where you come in. I've got a theory—you take what you're reading right now and use the ellipses…anywhere you want. Start from there with whatever comes to mind and don't stop, just keep going, and maybe, just maybe, you'll siphon off some of this attention, whatever's got me in its bull's eye, diffuse it a little, you know? I understand there's a risk, but maybe if you get a few others to do the same thing it won't land directly on you—march in step!—maybe we'll open some doors we didn't know were there, and maybe then, who knows, I'll get out of here. It's worth a try. I know you have little incentive to believe me. I wouldn't believe me. And the consequences are an X factor. And if it works, it makes you responsible for me for life.

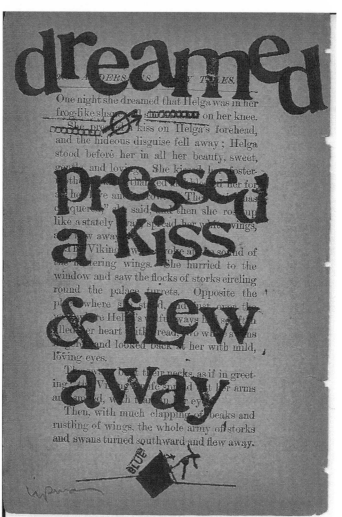

Joel Lipman

R. Bennett

Auricle / Ventricle

12 January, 1972

Editor
Saint Louis Post-Dispatch
Saint Louis, Missouri

Dear Editor,

I am writing to you from Amesly Hospital, Magruder Wing for the Blind, the free of mind, the sore of hind--no frigging. I have become adept at typing, but of course I can't see any spelling errors. Plus, I have a hangnail today, on my thumb (numb Tom). So if any typographs appear, I trust you will excuse them. When I have finished, I will call the nurse (erst most thrust), give her ten dollars and ask her to post my letter, as she has done for me so many times before. But I am growing weary (Druid floater). I am at the end of my tether, at the ether of my bother. No one will listen to me, hissen. My family thinks I am delusioned, elusive, allusive. They are too polite to call me "insane." They are too uptight to draw knee cranes. Nekkid spin. I don't like your attitude!

Listen, Mister, I have stolen a steak knife from the kitchen, serrated mastix. 1 have hidden a book of matches under my--well I won't tell you that. So there. Not yet. Do you think I sound irrational? Illogical? Quigley, even? Do you know that Lewis Carol often invited children to listen naked to his tales, all mumsy? And Charles Manson called candy "zu-zus." I'm sorry. So tarry. Please listen (hissen. I will tell you true...

In June, cool-spoon, following a series of stomach cramps, torrid bumpus, I entered the hospital for a hernia surgery. My surgeon, whose name I cannot reveal (tentative non-meal) for reasons that will soon be more than obvious, devious, told me that following the anesthesia, I would feel a bit weak for a day or so, dry-mouthed maybe (mucous dessicus), then return to "A-l prime condition." Oh, Herod! Oh, Pernod! Lord, the signs were there... I should have known, should have seen--hindsight is always so simple, as female nether is so ample. For instance, the surgeon had unusually long fingernails, glassene cuticus. They were over a half-inch and filed into sharp triangular points, rex-extensors. And clotted tufts of thick waxy black hair grew out of his ears. A small amount of wax is secreted by the male honey bee, from his "slake," a hollow tongue-like appendage used for peristalsis.

Did you know, in this "modern" day, in this protean society, we are so respectful of doctors. We worship them and pay them too well. They are walking gods--HARK! My nurse just came coming into the room. She is such a peach. Her skin has no peach hair like human skin. She is patting, rubbing, rutting my back now. I am getting an erection-protrusion. Perhaps I can cunnive this wondrous odiferous palmly creature with rustling blouse and non-malodourous armpit to do a little typing for me, pray tell? I will keep my pants on. I will not bait the master woodman, Mr. Hoodman...

[I am typing upon request of the patient --NB]

So I didn't dare protest the words of my doctor. I never second-guessed his odd use dashes--sadistic, I see now--request. He asked me to begin the surgery without any anesthesia. He wanted me to enter the operating room without being "pre-sedated" as they say. He told me that would be better for my heart.

I trusted him, of course. I looked up from the chrome-plated hospital bed and gazed into his porcine [spelling?] eyes. He wore thick spectacles back then. The glass was almost an inch-thick on the right lens, a half-inch on the left. When you stared straight into his eyes it was like looking through a microscope. You've done that before, haven't you, precious? Yes, you could see the black irises of course dash--but more, you could see the blood vessels in the whites of his right eye, throbbing like peat worms, lubriform. The left lens glinted an odd color, a sickly yellow, and when I peered deeper, I saw a cloudy form over the pupil. A cataract ... [I will try to slip in a few words (typist).]

But I followed the doctor's advice. I didn't fret, and indeed remember feeling rather calm as an orderly wheeled me into the operating room, a warm towel draped across my thighs, another across my chest. My wrists were buckled to the sides of the gurney. A minute later, an enormous lamp the size of a bureau mirror was glaring down, searing, spearing into my face. A moist film gathered on my forehead, which was odd. I never perspire; that's one of my best qualities. Can't you tell? [I am Nancy Balkin, Registered Nurse. This patient is not dangerous, but he-]

"Don't worry," said the doctor, "It's just like a dream..." He laughed and told the orderly to leave the room. Then he took out a syringe and a vial to prepare the intravenous solution. He asked my weight and height. He inserted the needle--an elaborately large needle it seemed, as for a horse or a steer, or a beefalo--deep into the blue vein below my biceps. I turned my head at the last moment. I've always been a bit squeamish. They used to tease me in grade school, when I wouldn't hold the class garter snake... [Truthfully, he has been diagnosed as clinically paranoid and a mild schizophrenic, but he is highly intelligent, and creative--I must stop now. He will count hammer strokes...]

The doctor leaned forward, licked his bottom lip, and adjusted his glasses on the bridge of his nose, septum-semitic. "Do you have twenty-twenty vision?" he asked.

I suppose in general it wasn't such an odd question. But in view of the fact that I was in the hospital to have my appendix out, I wondered what my vision could possibly matter. I figured it must have something to do with the type of anesthetic he was administering... How it affected the visual centers the of the brain, the optic nerves--I don't know. I'm not a scientist, no herpetologist's opthalmologist. I just didn't give it a second thought. [You can contact the Amesly Hospital administration office if you are ever threatened by this patient. He has been known to send bomb threats. I must admit, though, he's narrating an interesting story so far...]

"You must imagine something very beautiful," he told me. "Just as you start to feel the drug taking you under, think about a pretty landscape, a beach or a field of flowers... While you are asleep, you will have no conception of time. And when you awake, your last memory will be one of a lovely vision."

I thought of the grand canyon, pink ravines, bottomless chasms; a lone brown hawk flying, circling down through the air currents into the depths. [He has written various letters to the editors of newspapers, but none have responded. So you shouldn't feel obligated to.]

Then the tips of my fingers began to tingle, and the soles of my feet as well. My eyelids drooped, although I fought to keep them open for a final glance, optic-scoop, at the fluorescent tubes of the surgical lamp, the pale green walls, the rows of gleaming scalpels, scissors, pincers--and, curiously, a box of toothpicks--on the operating tray. Just before I fell asleep, out of the slits of my eyes, I saw my doctor lean down. His beaked nose, tip rosette, almost touched my cheek as he whispered to me in a low voice, words which now have burned their insidious memory in my head: "Red, carmine, scarlet," he hissed. "Crimson, ruby wine, oxygenated auricular P-venous... " [I'm sorry. He constantly speaks of his penis. We're used to it, though. I'm sure you've noticed that I'm trying to edit out his babble and make this letter coherent. I write a bit myself, actually!]

I tried to twist away from him, to roll to the side on the table, but the anesthetic had taken hold, pinned me like a vice. My legs were leaden, my arms paralyzed. And, although with all my might, physical effort and mental conviction, lifting up with the muscles of my forehead, I fought the final closure of my eyes, it was futile. They shut as if by tremendous force of gravity. But I was conscious for a few moments longer, before I sank. I was aware for a few seconds more of my doctor's voice in my ear, his mumbled words and smacking lips. I will tell you exactly what he said, word for word--I swear, with my good thumb over my heart: "Oh Belial!" he moaned. "Oh Lucifer, Diabolus, Rictus, Locus, Scrotious Satan--enter us now. Take us, feed us, as we have planned..." [I write stories about the nurses and doctors on staff here. They're very good. I read them over and over to myself (and my cat), and they're always really interesting and exciting, if you know what I mean... I sent one to REDBOOK, and they didn't need it at the time, but said it showed "real promise"!]

After these words, I lost consciousness. Total immersion, a deadened elephantine sleep, for a few minutes at least. But gradually I became aware again--not alert in the usual way, but cognizant on some level. I knew the operation was taking place, the scalpel in my stomach, the clamp against folds of abdominal skin; suction hose of fluid, excised stricken appendix, flaccid phallus... Yes, I understood this, but sensed more. I saw, if you could call it that, much further. The vision was nothing of an earthly type, the view not terrestrial. It was ur-sensual. Do you know that word, my dear? I experienced a fusion of two bright colors, a divided field, a floating mass of hue. On top was blue, crystalline light of a pure and transparent quality parentheses robin egg), yet seeming to extend upward to infinity. Below this, at roughly mid-level from my point of perception, was a thick hazy reddish zone, a mixture of vermillion light and jagged patches of rust, scabular. I scanned down and the redness deepened, formed patterns, sections, serpentine lines--a lizard's tail, an insect's leg, and a row of leaping flames, which oddly produced no smoke. [Perhaps you'd be more interested in reading some of MY stories? I have a whole collection, which I refer to as the "Balkin Bunch"--isn't that a cute name! In my latest story, Doctor Felix, who occurs in most of my tales, discovers that Nurse Freda has been shaving her legs with the surgical knives (to get super smooth) and then re-sterilizing them--]

I felt myself hovering outside both of these realms, the red and the blue, but pressured forward, pushed ahead, so that I was no longer beyond them but now at their perimeter, almost in their midst. And at some basal, primeval level, I knew that I would be forced to choose. That inevitably I would progress ahead, be driven onward, but that I would have some control over vertical motion; I could ascend into the filtered blue light, or I could sink and float down into the red, which now seemed to tug at my loins, to pull me from within. [My story takes place on Valentine's day. Dr. Felix has a tie with red hearts--which matches his newly-creased boxer shorts. But of course you don't learn this until later. I mean, my stories always have lots of suspense!]

"Are you listening?--" [oops, mistake--don't tell him]. But as I tried to "swim" upwards, the best verb I can conjure to describe the motion involved, as I tried to attain the blue atmos [?], there rose in front of me an obstacle, a writhing black mass, flailing filial strands. Then the mound rotated slowly, degree by degree, and it became clear that the strands were in fact hairs--long black hairs, over a profile, a face on the other side--a nose, a sneer colon: the visage of my doctor, hair askew, forehead wrinkled and scarred, red keloid lines crossing his brow at odd angles, forming--and my heart pulsed; upon the doctors brow, cast in puffy ridges of lineal scars was emblazoned an inverted pentagram, a baphomet, the top angles bent like goat horns. [Dr. Felix really is an old goat. He has a goaty forehead, with bumps over his eyes. When he catches Nurse Freda shaving her legs, he bends over and says that he has to rub her calves to make sure that the surgeon's knives are sharp...]

The marred face loomed in front of me, gleaming eyes, a reddish aura. Then a prickly schlierian [spelling?] force like thousands of fork tines drove me backwards, downwards, away from the cool blue region. Two clawed hands dug into the crown of my head. I was plunged further below, into the red mire. And I felt it in the pit of my stomach as I sank--raw guilt, a cutting pain as if I had been caught in flagrant adultery; yet accompanied by a genital satisfaction,____-lust [expletive deleted, (N. B.)], as if I were still in the midst of fornication... Soon I could no longer propel myself at all, felt an utter loss of will, and merely sank deeper, into what now was patently a blaze of fire--but cold somehow. Freezing. The ice-fire of Hades. It exists, you know. I have seen it. [But see, Freda really has a crush on Felix (because he's rich and has two Mercedes), and she grasps his big hand with her two warm little hands and presses his face to her you-know-what. (This is really steamy stuff I write. It's not for kids.) And Freda is very hot, where it matters. But Doctor Felix's hand is cold as ice, so she presses her creamy thighs together to warm it up, and--]

When I awoke, I was groggy, uncertain at first if I wasn't still in fact under the ether, or in some other sopor, with a total lack of saliva in my mouth, a dry tongue that stuck to the inside of my cheeks, adhesive gluteous, and an aching burning need for water. I swallowed. My tonsils clung in my throat.

"How are we?" I heard the nurse's voice. Soft fingers parted my lips and placed upon my swollen tongue an ice cube, a wonderful thing, its cool melt soothing, refreshing as no other. "We can't give you any tap water right after the surgery--you might choke on your vomit," she said sweetly. [And while Doctor and Freda are together, she starts to sing to him, the theme from "Dr. Doolittle," which is her favorite song, and she always dreamed of marrying a doctor and never getting divorced, and having a son named "Fred," and a daughter named "Francesca." So Freda undoes Dr. Felix's fly, which isn't stuck, and she starts to think about living with him forever, which is what she always thinks about with a man before she makes love. She is getting wet and--]

I managed a real swallow, flexed my fingers, and for the first time tried to open my eyes--but adhesive tape, a bandage was wrapped over my nose, down past my ears, around my head. I lifted two hands and tried to touch it, but felt the crisp gauze and hard cotton padding over my cheeks. Curiously, it was a firm mold as if caked in plaster, still hot as it set. [A competent nurse would not allow the patient's filthy fingers on a fresh bandage. Especially a patient like this, who frequently masturbates, to be totally honest. Several of the night attendants have reported it in the log book.]

"Now don't touch the bandage!" came the nurse's voice, chiding, as if she were speaking to a small child. She pulled my hands back. [So anyway, Dr. Felix tries to touch Nurse Freda's you-know-what again, with three fingers this time, but she pushes his hands back, because now she's playing hard-to-get...]

"Why do I have a bandage over my eyes?" I heard myself ask--a hoarse voice from an invalid's throat. I tried to sit up, to wrench my shoulders forward. A leather belt dug into my chest, held me down. "I had my appendix out--a stomach operation. It's got nothing to do with my eyes..." My voice cracked. I coughed and choked on my own stale tongue.

"Doctor will explain everything to you when you're more relaxed... He's very busy now." She paused, caught her breath "--Oh, there he is. Doctor... Doctor...," she called to him softly, as if addressing a minister, a master. "Oh, Doctor, don't forget your spectacles." [But Freda accidently leaves her underpants in the sterilizing room, in with the hospital gowns, and then the head nurse finds them. See, everybody always thought the head nurse was mean, a tough Bossy-Betty, but then we find out that she really likes Freda, and wants to bed down with her--but just embrace. No monkey biz.]

1 heard his voice then. The same voice that had explained the operation to me; informed me about the anesthesia. But now there was a new timbre, a deep rasp, almost a growl--a stab in my chest. I saw the image of the doctor's pock-marked forehead, raised baphomet scar points above treacherous yellow eyes. "Just hold the spectacles for me, nurse," he said. "I won't be needing them right now."

"But you always wear them--" she began in a matronly scold and then quickly cut herself off, as if she had spoken out of place, broken a tacit agreement. Perhaps the doctor had given her his stare... [He's right. A good nurse will never speak back to Doctor.]

Suddenly, the bed wobbled, flapped on the floor. My feet swayed in front of me above a swelling blanket. I could feel the sutures in my stomach, an itching pressure, deep incision, a narrow burn. I was exhausted, and I yearned for the light of day. [The head nurse smells semen on Freda's panties, which smell curiously like Camembert cheese, so she takes it to the lab and has it analyzed, then compares the results to staff blood-type data--we're a modern hospital!]

The doctor himself peeled the bandage off my face. His fingers were cold, as if he had just numbed them in snow. The adhesive tape tugged at the skin and tiny hairs of my cheeks, but eventually tore free. The bandage was lifted off my nose--I blinked. Blinked again. "I--I can't see," I told him. "It's all black, it's..." And then I shouted, screamed like a child lost in a cave, "I can't see anything!"

His hand gripped my shoulder. The sharp points of his fingernails pierced my skin even through the hospital gown. "Your appendectomy went very well," he told me in a low voice. "But your nervous system atrophied under general anesthesia--a very rare occurrence. Your vision might return. We'll have to runs more tests, and... "

My neck throbbed. "You took my eyes!" I almost spat, tried to pull myself up, to wriggle out into the dark. The belt cut into my abdomen. "You stole my eyes," I shrieked. "I know that's why you don't need your spectacles now. I saw you! I SAW YOU IN HELL!" I lunged at him then, at his voice in the blackness, but caught only air in my hands, held only my own cold, damp fingers in my fists.

Feet pounded across the floor. Two big palms pressed against my chest, shoved me down on the mattress. Another gloved hand dug into my lips, silenced my screams. I writhed, thrashed my head, tried to bite at the hard bitter leather, but knuckles slipped into my mouth, against my teeth and gums. A pain like a wasp sting--another needle was jabbed into my arm much more roughly than before. "Twelve hundred milligrams," the doctored ordered, in his fiendishly calm voice. "He's hallucinating..." [So the head nurse is in a rage. She can barely see straight. She is forcing her big self to remain calm, while her feet pound down the halls...]

They transferred me to the mental ward temporarily, agrarily, merrily. That's aways their ultimate solution. I rebelled, yes--at first. But I soon learned that my screams, my ravings and accusations brought only more medication--and less frequent changing of the bed pan, I'm not sure which was worse. After a few months, upon threats of permanent assignment to the lunatic ward, I recanted my charges of devilry, hell tract, hell hyphen tract, against the doctor. I made a show of being a contrite patient, a model inmate. I washed my face sixteen times a day. I combed my hair, de-snare. I tied my shoes. I used my napkin at the table. Foldy nappy on my lips.

After a year of observation I was allowed to enter the Magruder Wing, for rehabilitation and Braille training. I practiced bird calls (I can make a pigeon's warble). I practiced my typing all day long, but I am not nearly as good as my lovely nurse... [He can be sweet when he wants to, the poor blind old yak. So anyway then, here's the climax of my story: The next week, the head nurse finds Freda and Dr. Felix groping in a supply closet. Dr. Felix has his shirt undone revealing his smooth muscular chest and tight, firm abdomen, because he works out at a gym. Expertly he unsnaps Freda's Cross-Your-Heart brassiere. Freda breathes quickly, and allows Felix's hand to glide gently down the silky insides of her round, firm breasts, with erect aq;wdlkfaW-RRRRRRRRRWT

...You will probably see, Mister E., that the typing has changed, because my odiferous nurse has deserted me, after--and I admit no evil by grasping her warm rubinesque mildly bovine hooters as she was typing.... Her breaths had become abnormally short and fast, like panting and I even heard a moan. Telepathically, she requested my action triad. But then she ran out, howling feline, crooning "Felix," and I fear the doctor will arrive here soon. I must type quickly, fixedly...

As I sit here now, a sacred glass-eyed dour, it is not entirely dark. Sometimes I see odd nuances, traces or what I take to be flashes of light. Perhaps they are only my imagination. When I can't sleep, I conjure up images, scenes from the past, and run them through my mind like a moving picture--a talkee, even. At least I can do this mein herr. Some of my fellow patients--the liver-lipped drools, glad bag of stools--have never seen anything at all. I try, hopelessly, to explain the world to them. I used to be a teacher, before that a preacher-beseecher... But really, perhaps they are better off, above the frey, cliff-dwellers. They are not tortured like I am, by what they have lost. They are not haunted by a doctor's scurvied face, by the deeds of a man who has lain with the devil, copulated against thorns, horn-sodomizing.

I make no pretense to know what you, sitting in your padded desk chair, might possibly do to help me now. I know not how, through prayer or sorcery, to seek my vengeance, in the essence or in the abstract of the conundrum, O fang-filched cross!! As I blindly type this last sheet of paper; as I hear the keys hammering very near the bottom of the page--the noise is higher pitched against the platen (surgus)--deafening, I am begging for your help. I plead for your assistance. Do not desert me!!! Or I will find you. I've seen your face, even without my eyes.

Eternally

Yours

Adam Peterson

The Grandmas Dream of Revolution

When the grandpas die, so too do the dreams of RVs and great-grandchildren, the memories of vacations and pear blossoms, the grandmas' faith in things getting better.

The grandmas wake before the sun with a bitter taste slowing their tongues. They open their eyes to the empty side of the bed and remember what goodness will never return to the country. Not unless they do something about it.

They resolve to do something about it.

So they wake even earlier with chants of freedom in their mouths, see visions of eagles and Idaho, feel their faith in the Imperial measuring system stronger than before.

The grandmas descend on the nation's capital. They park their old Buicks in Virginia and ask for directions to the president. Station agents help them onto trains and groaning teenagers give up their seats on the bus after the grandmas complain of tired feet.

The teenagers will regret this kindness most of all.

Drawn by the smell of lavender and butterscotch, the grandmas find each other on the Mall. They wave quilted placards reading *I ♥ Hating America* on the front and *I miss Earl* on the back. They trade recipes for homemade explosives. They make cutting remarks about Debra's ex-husband.

A congressman takes the grandmas to lunch. Before he begins, he asks if they can all hear him okay, and for this the grandmas take their purses and politely beat him to death.

The grandma's are sick of this shit.

The grandmas light the restaurant on fire. The grandmas tip over the Washington Monument. The grandmas occupy Ford's Theatre.

Now when they wake, they taste blood, and though there's someone beside them for the first time since Clarence went, instead of a shared life they see a slow death for America.

The president resists—at first.

But then the grandmas ask why he never calls and if he's still dating Sally and wasn't Sally a bit stuck-up and do you think she's put on weight and the president resigns.

At first, it's better with the grandmas. Everyone wakes up in time to watch the sunrise. Bridge games abound. Hard candy replaces virulent online discourse.

And though the grandmas refuse to hold an election, everyone votes for them anyway with birthday cards reading, _Sorry this is late, Bubbe!_ Even The Supreme Court rules that after long, meaningful lives, the grandma's have earned a little junta, and that Betty shouldn't have to put up with all she does from that boy.

But the grandmas run out of dreams.

The morning comes when they can taste nothing, can see nothing, cannot imagine ever having had faith in anything at all. The grandmas unknit their sweaters and walk naked to greet their subjects, saying, *My child, what did we do?*

And no one knows if this is the end or only an ending.

The Long Lake Dream

The Mortgage Man looms through the foggy glass of the porch door again.

"Come in," I say. "I want you to come in."

I open the old door, with its flaking black paint and swiss-cheesed screen, and it sways like a windchime in the autumn breeze as he steps inside.

"No, I don't want your card," I say when he reaches for his breast pocket, and "Wait right there a moment, I have to let the dog in." I open the porch's opposite door, also dangling, and beckon for Haley, a smiling Alaskan Malamute, who kicks up mud and red leaves as she dashes into my waiting hands. I undo the clip on her chain, and she bolts to the back door, rattling its brass doorknob. The Mortgage Man looks at me blankly. I ignore him and open the door to the kitchen, which Haley bursts through with a clatter of nails on tile, before hooking a left into the living room and disappearing.

The man and I step into the kitchen and he goes for his card again. "Honestly," I say, putting a hand in his face: "That's enough. I know you. You are with Carrington Mortgage, and your big red truck, from which you just took pictures of every angle of our house, is parked on the street. You've come in to tell us you're foreclosing; you are going to act as though we've never talked before." I pat him on the shoulder. "But I've seen you dozens of times – in my dreams and otherwise. So just come in. I'll give you the tour. You can leave your shoes on. I know that, to you, none of this is real."

There is a pattering of footsteps, and two little kids burst into the kitchen. They run directly toward us, and when the Mortgage Man holds out his hand to stop them, I laugh. The kids run into him, phasing through his khaki pants. "That one is me," I say, pointing to the taller one, who is reaching for the cupboards, "And that is my brother

Nicky," I say, pointing to the shorter one with shocking blue eyes, who rummages through the drawers. The Mortgage Man and I watch as Young Nicky and Young Me find a half-loaf of bread in a drawer, the wood of which is stained dark with the cigarette smoke redolent in the air, with the dirt in the grooves from our little fingers. Young Me drops two slices of bread into the plastic toaster, its white corners melted in little tears down the sides. The Mortgage Man and I watch Young Nicky open the fridge, filled with stains and spills but very little food, and grab a cube of butter and a couple green apples. There's a clattering behind us, and we turn around to watch Young Me standing at the sink, pushing aside empty plastic bottles of UV Blue vodka, rinsing a thin dust of ash from a mason jar before filling it with water, then beckoning Young Nicky over to the oven, where a chair sits. The two stand on it, little feet shuffling to make room, and they stare into the heat-warped mirror on the spice cabinet above the stovetop, laughing at and trying to make sense of their distorted images – the eyes stretched like putty, cheekbones swooping to their chins.

The toast pops. The Mortgage Man jumps.

"Anyway," I say, clapping his shoulder, "That is basically the kitchen." I wave for him to follow me into the dining room, and as we cross the tiles, we see the bathroom door slightly open in our periphery, through which we can see Pre-Teen Me, built like a scarecrow, staring ponderously at a stick of deodorant. We can see the mold climbing up the shower curtain, and lazy cobwebs in the corners. Pre-Teen Me realizes the door is open, and he closes it before we see anything else.

We walk through the kitchen to the dining room now, and as our figures pass through the haze of cigarette smoke, the Mortgage Man pulls a letter from his back pocket and tries to shove it in front of me. Without looking, I grab the letter from his hand and frisbee it into a milkcrate, which overflows with newspapers and other such letters near the woodstove that glows orange, the radiant heat of which splits the stacked maple and pine logs on the hearth. My mom, her cigarette burning but seeming never to shrink, sits at the dining room table and stares out the window, maybe at the birds in the grass, or at the shining Long Lake across the street, beyond the neighbors' yards. Beneath her is Haley, who licks at the plates that my mom simply places on the floor when she is done with them.

At the far end of the table is Teenage Me playing a game of chess. Some of the pieces are replaced with random objects: there are batteries for rooks, a crayon for a queen. Across the board is another teenage boy, a little shorter, more filled out, with a head of brown, frazzled hair. "That's Chance," I tell the Mortgage Man. "I met him in first grade." There are pink, ring-like scars almost glowing on Chance's forearms. The Mortgage Man stares, and I say, "That was his biological mom, putting cigarettes out on his arms when he was little." The Mortgage Man blinks. "That's unfortunate," he says.

"Don't even get me started on his dad," I say, as Teenage Me shakes his head and buries his face in his hands as Chance checkmates him with a drained double-A on the back rank.

The Mortgage Man and I step past my dazed mom and take the little leap from the dining room to the office. This room is cold, too. Our breath puffs visibly in the air. In the middle of the carpet, Teenage Nicky, Chance, and Me, thin fighting gloves strapped to our hands, wrestle clumsily, throw wild punches, basically try to beat the shit out of each other. The Mortgage Man backs away from the scrum. I laugh a little and say, "Almost every younger guy around here, the ones in town and in the trailers in the woods, want to be prize fighters. Almost all of them on the school bus have said so. Isn't that strange?" Teenage Me buckles to an uppercut in the solar plexus from Teenage Nicky. "It's funny," I say, looking at the Mortgage Man. "It's like we're all angry, or something."

We turn to leave the office, but the outside door behind us opens, and a gust of air, and a wash of light, fill the room. Standing behind us is a teenage girl, holding a stack of clothes. She raises her eyebrows at the boys and says, "What are you guys *doing?*"

The Mortgage Man and I step out of the office, back to the warmth of the dining room. "That was Savanah," I tell him, "She lives in the big house across the field." As we walk back through the dining room, a Pre-Teen Me is wrestling on the floor with Haley, who has the big paws and oversized ears and high-pitched grumble of a dog not-fully-grown. My mom, with bright eyes and strong posture sits in her chair at the head of the table and watches and laughs. The chessboard sits on the end of the table, all pieces present and in-position.

When we enter the living room, it is suddenly nighttime.

In front of the buzzing, square television, my dad cradles a Playstation controller in his hands as he rocks an unsleeping baby in the wicker rocking chair. The console at his feet hums, spins a game called *Metal Gear Solid* hundreds of times a minute. Solid Snake, main character, presses flat to a metal cargo crate; on his left, a guard, white-uniformed and clueless, puffs a dozen pixelated breaths into the snowy air before turning around, walking away on one of his many predestined routes.

"That's me," I whisper to the Mortgage Man, pointing to the baby in my dad's arms. This is our first year in the house, my first year anywhere. The unfamiliar cold of northern Wisconsin infiltrates through the unfinished windows, spreads goosebumps like a rash over my dad's arms. A single, white-shaded lamp illuminates the corner of the room, casts the cracks of the floorboards and the ceiling in contrast to the moon through the window. The room smells of creosote, which sits, fuming and jagged, freshly evicted from the chimney, in paper bags strewn everywhere around the largely unfurnished house. Baby Me fusses in my dad's arms as he embodies Solid Snake, as he knocks on walls and leaves false footprints in the snow to distract the guards, as he procures a handgun and crawls through a ventilation shaft into the hangar of the nuclear-weapon disposal facility of Shadow Moses Island, near Alaska.

"It's a great game," I whisper to the Mortgage Man. "It was revolutionary, you know. For being the first game where you need to be stealthy, instead of just blowing everyone away." The Mortgage Man only nods slowly in the dark. "It's not that macho American shit," I say. "It's considered a quintessential piece of 20th century art." The Mortgage Man only blinks. On the screen, Solid Snake sets a cardboard box over his head and waits for a guard to pass him by.

"Anyway," I say. "Look," and I point to the couch, where a young man lies flat on his back, blanket twisted around his body, which is stiff as a corpse. "That's me," I whisper to the Mortgage Man. He stands over my sleeping body, stares at my frozen form. "Like the real me, right now," I whisper. On the TV screen, Solid Snake grabs a guard from behind and snaps his neck. The guard's body drops to the snow, flickers three times, then disappears.

"Do you know what sleep paralysis is?" I ask the Mortgage Man. He shakes his head. I lean into his ear, and whisper: "In the old days, they called it 'an intercepting of the motion of the voice and respiration.' And that's exactly right," I say. "You cannot move – not even to shift your eyes from left to right. But you're awake – your mind is awake, but because you're paralyzed, because of the fear that comes when you can't even twitch, you're having a nightmare." The Mortgage Man keeps staring at the sleeping me. "When people report seeing ghosts or demons in their room," I say, "When they think someone has snuck into their home, it is often a symptom of sleep paralysis."

The Mortgage Man blinks. "That's unfortunate," he says, without breaking his gaze.

"You get what I'm saying, right?" I say to him. Gunshots ping from the television. The first boss of *Metal Gear*, Revolver Ocelot, reloads his six-shooter.

"That's you," I say to him. "The monster I manifest in the worst of my dreams."

Revolver Ocelot, in his scary voice, says as he spins the cylinder of his revolver, *"I love the smell of cordite...you know, that sulphury smell?"*

We turn from the living room and immediately Pre-Teen Savanah and Pre-Teen Me open a door to our right and run up the stairs, giggling as they pass through our bodies. I thought about taking The Mortgage Man up that twisting staircase, the steps of which had tufts of Haley fur stuffed into their corners. I could have told the Mortgage Man endlessly about the patches of drywall in our rooms that would crumble from the angled ceiling in a sudden heap, about the nests of little sweatpants and torn jeans I would make for the bats that sometimes swirled through the room, for the mice that skittered through the drawers and across the floor. I could have told him about the insulation from the edges of the window that spilled out in fine hairs into the dark, and how in my sleepiest moments I'd sometimes jolt up in panic, thinking it was the hair of some monster, some intruder. But for all the times the Mortgage Man was the looming intruder, I felt he already knew.

I pat the Mortgage Man hard on the shoulder. I gesture to a slightly open door next to the door upstairs, my mom's room, and lead him in there.

In her room, it is daytime again. Haley, fully-grown, rolls about on the bed, kicking up dust that dances in the gentle pressure of the sun. She stops her thrashing and looks at herself, upside down, in the vanity of my mom's dresser. The Mortgage Man and I pass our ghostly feet through hundreds and hundreds of cigarettes and stained tissues that have overflowed from a wastebin next to the bed. Cobwebbed pictures of Nicky and I as babies sit hang on the wall, thick brown insulation stains from the crack along the ceiling run down the image of our faces.

I beckon the Mortgage Man into my mom's closet. He joins me, and our legs phase through my dad's old hunting coats, my mom's old dresses. I point to a shelf over our heads. I watch the Mortgage Man's eyes search, search, and go huge when they land at what I'm pointing at. It is the only thing not covered in dust. In fact, it shines by the light of the bare bulb hanging from the ceiling. The Mortgage Man takes a step back.

It is the gun. It is the handgun my dad grabs every time the Mortgage Man's red truck with "CARRINGTON" spelled out on the side comes around, the gun that he sighs before grabbing, the gun he holds at his side when he marches right toward the glinting lens of the camera in the Mortgage Man's hands. It is the gun that puts that truck in reverse and sends it flying down the road.

I turn and look into the Mortgage Man's wide eyes. I want to tell him so much. That, all my life, he was the shape that snuck through the door, that hovered over me in my bed when I'd be half there, and half not. As a kid and even now, I searched through every stack of mail for his company's yellow notices, that I've always grown nauseous when I see the name "Carrington." For as long as I can remember, he's been trying to evict us from our home. And I want to evict him from existence.

Instead, I take a deep breath, and I sigh it out. I say, "Let's get some fresh air." I gesture for him to follow me back through my mom's room, where now an Adult Nicky and Adult Me in dust masks shovel hundreds and hundreds of cigarette butts, nested in piles and piles of black ash, into paper bags with dust pans, and a Haley with grey in her fur takes two tries to jump on the bed next to Mom, who sits upright, head tipped into her shoulder, tucked away into a dream of her own.

On the TV screen in the living room, Solid Snake stands over a bleeding Sniper Wolf, the legendary marksman loved by the wolf dogs scattered about the Alaskan island. They generate little pixel hearts over their head at the sight of her gasping body. In this way, she's the hardest boss to kill. My dad sets the controller gently in his lap as she says, in a cutscene, *"...okay hero. Set me free."*

"You know," I say, turning to the Mortgage Man as we walk back through the dining room, towards the kitchen. "Those old games, the big ones, like *Metal Gear*, that tell a whole world-saving story, that render all those details – they used to be too big to fit onto one disc. At some point in the story," I say, "You'd have to switch discs. And the good games, they knew just how to time that switch, knew when to cut the screen to black so you'd be staring at your own gawking face in the reflection, you know? Right between the peak of chaos and the moment your character decides to fix it all."

We take one step further into the kitchen, and the bathroom door opens to our side. The light changes, and my Mom, younger, is there suddenly, opening the door to reveal Haley, no bigger than a bundled sweater, who toddles across the tiles of the kitchen and wanders into Young Nicky and Young Brandon's arms as they shake with joy. They bury their face in her thick fur. She looks at them with the big brown eyes of a doe.

I take a deep breath. I beckon the Mortgage Man through the back door, out to the porch, where we walk right through a downtrodden Adult Savanah, carrying a bundle of flowers.

We step outside into the crunching leaves of our shedding basswood tree. A clunking Oldsmobile pulls up into the driveway. Dad, younger, fuller, with dark, long hair, swings open the driver's door, runs to the passenger door, and opens it up. He reaches in, and helps lift out my Mom, who is in a back brace, knee brace, and shoulder cast, whose blue eyes are squeezed shut from the punch of an airbag, which I know, but the Mortgage Man does not know, activated in a puff of dust when her Jeep flipped on an icy road, and she twisted her spine, shattered her hip, dislocated her knee, broke her ribs, ended her career, and lost the seven-month bump in her belly that would have been my little sister – a little girl she wanted to name

"Haley," Teenage Me whispers from beside us, in the backyard, where The Mortgage Man and I turn and look now to see Teenage Nicky and Teenage Me shakily sink to our knees, and hug Haley's frail body, with her sparse hair and sunken eyes, the thin waist and inflamed hips of a long life. The Mortgage Man and I watch as my dad, who stands over us, pats us on the shoulders, then coaxes Haley to follow him.

The Mortgage Man and I look back and my parents are gone, and back again and the teenage boys are gone, too. There is only my dad and the autumnal wind and Haley. His handgun dangles from his fingers, he is crying for the first and only time I've ever seen. He takes her to the woods in the back, in the midst of a grove of birch trees, towering and beautiful and speckled black and white just like her. He sets her gently in that grave we dug, and he pets her between the ears before he stands up straight, wipes his tears, aims the gun, and sets her free.

--------------------INSERT DISC 2--------------------

It is very still. It is very still on Long Lake in all of my dreams. The Mortgage Man groans, then blinks awake.

We float in the canoe that my dad bought from someone in the village that rings the lake, years ago, just after he and my mom had me, just after they bought the house. The canoe that Chance and Nicky and I learned how to seal shut with rivets, learned how to furnish with seats cut with a reciprocating saw and stained with the same old stain my dad used for the floors of our home. It was the very canoe I took Savanah on dozens of fishing trips with, that housed us as we pulled in the marvels of life beneath the water and let them go, the vessel that let us be one with the lake that we would see gleaming through the window when we would lie together in my bedroom, that we'd taste in the air when we went outside to pick crab apples in the yard or just sit in the dewy grass. The Mortgage Man and I float on an invisible current past my neighbors' yards, who live right on the lake, who Nicky and I cut grass and picked pinecones and raked leaves for as a kid in exchange for access to their pier. So that we could fish. So that we could dangle our feet in the water. We float past the big T-shaped pier that all the younger men in town put in together, a process that all the older men would watch while reminiscing about the times they were the ones in the chest-deep water, kicking their feet in the mud to find the poles to rest the pier's sections in. We float on Long Lake, as I do so often in my dreams.

"You know," I tell the Mortgage Man, "My dad, all his life, has wanted to visit Alaska." Red leaves drift from the trees around us, sway to the lake's surface. I huff a visible breath into the air. "But there was never the money. And he was too busy with us. With Mom after the accident, with scaring you off our street." I look at my hands, try to rub the cold from my fingers.

"Listen," I say to the Mortgage Man. "This is my home." The Mortgage Man nods, his expression blank.

"Maybe," I say, "it's true that it's just your job to try and kick us out of it when the checks don't come. Maybe you'll lose your own home if you don't take pictures of mine."

The Mortgage Man nods again. "It is unfortunate," he says.

I look out over the lake, at the mist on the cut of horizon, the trees going to sleep all along the shoreline. Little imperceptible fish kiss the surface, leave ripples everywhere. I sigh.

"It is," I say. "It really is."

And I push him out of the canoe.

I lunge and push him out of the canoe and he sinks into Long Lake, where maybe everything turns blue. Maybe after the explosion of bubbles he'll open his eyes, and he'll feel the exhilarating cold all over his skin, and the tiny fish like slivers of light will dash in every direction at his presence, and he'll sink and the bluegill and perch will look at him ponderously, and the tallest weeds will wrap around his body and grab the slack of his polo, of his khakis, and the very water will taste of life, and bleed the ink from his business cards, and the northern pike and largemouth bass will be drawn to his commotion, will swirl about him as he sinks in deeper, until the purple loosestrife and thick stems of lilies enclose him in a watery forest, and he'll only know up from down if he exhales a few bubbles to see which way they go. Maybe he'll settle into the mud with the bullheads and crayfish and all the other scavengers, and maybe in that mud he'll see years and years of things like dropped fishing poles or ice ladles, engine props and rusted tools and skipping rocks – maybe he'll see the little pocket knife I would use to cut clean lines on myself when he'd come around often, the one I threw with all my might from that T-shaped pier one day when I decided I wasn't afraid anymore, after Haley, the backbone of our home, was gone, and I knew it was my turn to fix everything. Maybe the Mortgage Man will land right next to that glinting knife in the watery blue, and maybe he'll feel something.

Or maybe not. I don't know. What I do know is that I'll break my sleep paralysis with a start and a gasp as always, and I'll awake in the sunlight in the living room, and while I won't see the big red bobber of him on the lake through the foggy window, I will see the red leaves scattered on its misty surface and chuckle at the thought that it's him, exploded into a million pieces.

I know that I'll slowly come to, and remember that even though I passed out on the couch like I always used to, I'm a somewhat grown man now, home for a visit. In my drowsy state I'll expect for a moment the happy clatter of Haley coming to wake me with a cold nose. And though I won't quite get that, my mom, fairly steady now, in the dining room, with its walls now cleaned of the layers of smoke and ash and little fingerprints, will wish me "Good morning." I know I will stand myself up, and today, Nicky and I will do some cleaning. We'll gut every cupboard of every item in the kitchen – every chipped plate, streaked cup, stained mug, cracked bowl, rusted pan, peeling pot, warped sheet, skewed fork, dull knife, and bent spoon, we'll lay in piles on the floor. We'll save the best handful of these things and throw the rest away, bags and bags of fractured glass, tired metal, Tupperware lids to nothing. And when we get tired, we'll settle in and play games for the night, and the peace will sneak up on us. The gun in the closet will collect more dust, the knife in the lake will sink further into the silt. And of course, there will be a point in the evening, when the light of the falling sun comes through the windows and lights the house in that amber way, that I'll look, just look, at our patchwork home. A quintessential piece of 20th century art. We'll play games that night and feel grateful for the heat of the fire, the single strands of Haley fur hidden in funny places like potted plants, or beneath the legs of couches. And just before dark, I'll stare out of one of those foggy, front-facing windows, that thin barrier that keeps me warm and frames perfectly the lake, my very favorite place.

**poem
come
with
me
morning
star**

Joel Lipman

Nathan Alling Long

The Table and Everything on It

It took me a while to understand where I was. I first thought I was at home, with my parents, my whole family, even my older brother, who had died at twenty-four in a motorcycle accident when I was seventeen. We were sitting around the table, Thanksgiving, or some holiday like it—Griefgiving I think someone called it, and we were all talking about what we didn't like about each other. We were going around the table and everyone decided to start with me.

I was small again, not only young, but short enough to barely see everyone's faces above the table, though old enough to understand their words.

Everyone was calm and soft spoken, but said the most terrible things. *You are greedy and unkind and steal from the change pot by the front door. You break into the bathroom when there are others in it. You didn't cry when Aunt Augusta died. You kill insects in the back yard and smile. You pee on yourself in the night. You touched the dog's penis when you thought no one was looking. You hoped your sister would break her leg when she fell off the playground equipment. You look over at your classmate's desk for answers to tests...*

On and on it went. They knew everything bad about me, even things there was no way they could know. I sat there, feeling smaller and smaller. My heart raced but at the same time, I couldn't feel it. It was like the ripple of a stone plunging into a lake, a soft, wavy echo of a heartbeat.

I am here, I told myself, *I am here.* But when I looked down, I seemed to become someone else, or maybe I was everyone. I suddenly could feel my sister's throat as she spoke of my faults, sin after sin, my mother's mouth, and my father's tongue. I heard my brother's voice as though it was my own.

I looked around the table again, and where I had thought various dishes of food were laid out—turkey and potatoes, beans and stuffing—there were only objects from my life that were evidence of my wrongs. My mother's tampons that I used to steal from the bathroom and pretend were hand grenades, pulling the string and tossing them across the yard. The clumps of white hair from the cat's one white patch, which I thought I could eliminate by pulling from his neck day after day. A model tank my brother had made and I had stolen and then broken the barrel of and then hid. And over there, my father's black belt on the back of which I had secretly written "I hate you" in pencil.

Dish after embarrassing dish were laid out before me, before us all, and everyone passed them around the table, taking the item and placing it on their plate, though it would somehow reappear on the serving dish again as it was passed to the next family member.

Soon, all the dishes were gathered around me, the only one at the table who didn't touch them, who wouldn't take from them, and refused to pass them on.

"It looks like you're hording them all," my sister said, shaking her head. "Why not take some and pass it on?"

It was then that my mother appeared with one more dish, a large black iron pot I'd never seen before. She was smiling as she set it down on the table with two oven mitts, and said, "Watch out, it's hot."

As my mother lifted the lid, my younger sister asked, "What is it?" The pot was full of a bubbling black liquid, like tar and ink boiling together.

"David knows what it is," my mother said and smiled at me. "It's there at the bottom." And then she lifted a ladle and submerged it into the boiling liquid and slowly drew the ladle up.

I both knew what it was and didn't know, a secret so dark I'd kept it even from myself, so no one would ever know it. I began to cry, hiding my eyes in my hands, wanting to run from the table, though I was unable to move my legs.

My brother, the one who died, laughed and said, "Crybaby."

In that word I understood what else he meant: What do you have to cry about? You weren't scrapped along a highway by a semi, your bones crushed, your skin torn off like tissue paper then soaked in blood, your fingers severed. You weren't in the hospital, after five surgeries, lying in some liminal state for days until you got an infection and died.

I took a deep breath and was about to cry again into my napkin, horrified that all the eyes of my family were on me, but a phrase my brother had suggested caught the edge of my thoughts. *Some liminal state.*

I said the words to myself, then took another breath, my face still wet, though I could not feel it, even as I pressed my hands against my skin.

I let my hands drop to my lap and looked up again. All the figures of my family began to hover as though they were ghosts, weightless in their chairs. The table itself floated, and all the dishes on it. I looked back down to see if I were doing the same. I examined my hands in my lap, but wherever I focused, they seemed to disappear. I could not be sure I was even in my body. Perhaps I was simply imagining it, because I'd always had one before.

When I looked back up, only my brother was left in the room. Even the table and everything on it had vanished. He was looking at me, nodding sympathetically now. It was as though he were saying, *Yes. Welcome.*

Susan A. H. Grace

Girl with Chrysanthemums

She can't have been more than ten. I thought so then; I think so now.

I had set out on a short walk to Ingrid's Market to buy apples, when I noticed a child standing alone in the alley between the pawn shop and the dry cleaner. I passed these stores, this alley, often on my way to pick up this or that from Ingrid's. I knew the area; I knew the people. This girl I'd never seen. I couldn't help but stop and stare, curious about her, about her circumstances: was she okay or in need of help or maybe lost? What a strange thing—a young girl with stems of white chrysanthemums clasped in her hands, her body rigid, her back to the alley wall, her face aimed straight ahead, as if posing for some invisible specter. All I could see was her profile. If she saw me peripherally she didn't acknowledge it. Beyond where she stood, mounds of trash spilled out of dumpsters—the stink ebbing and flowing at the mouth of the alley like the breath of a dying ogre. I would not have been shocked to see a rat sniffing at her shoes or a stray black cat twining through her legs. A loud horn jerked me from my reverie. A truck clearly there for a delivery needed to get through to one of the bays—a restaurant or perhaps Ingrid's further down the alley. I stepped aside, let him pass. The girl had vanished.

That evening my baby brother Theo and his girlfriend came to dinner. We had met the girlfriend only once at a small gathering to celebrate my dad's fifty-fifth birthday. That had been a couple of months back and I'd barely spoken to her—it was that kind of party, where everyone clamored to meet the girl who had stolen Theo's heart, which meant no one had time to get to know her, and my poor mother would later have to gather snippets of second-hand conversations to piece her together like a jigsaw puzzle.

"Damn, it smells good in here." Griff strolled into the kitchen while I was braising the meat, dropped his briefcase on the counter, wrapped his arms around me. He has these gorgeous almond-colored eyes and dark curly hair. His lips, even in his sleep, seem always to be smiling. Technically I think we're still newlyweds. We married a year ago last June right after Griff passed the bar. He had been offered lucrative positions with a couple of the status law firms in the city. He turned them all down to continue the work he'd started in his last two years of school—working with the wrongfully convicted. He'd been instrumental in exonerating three men and one woman. All three men were African American; the woman was white. The system had railroaded them into incarceration—collectively they'd spent 99 years in prison—but with new evidence, new DNA capabilities, lots of donations, and the dedication of dozens of attorneys, staff, students, one by one their innocence had been proven and they'd been set free.

"Rack of lamb, new potatoes, spinach and pear salad, cinnamon apples for dessert," I said. "Go get changed, then come back and you can open the wine, let it breathe."

Griff's suit I saw immediately was the same shade of gray as the girl's dress. His clothes nicely tailored; her dress large and ill-fitting. She must have noticed me, if only in her periphery, yet never once did she look my way. I saw her only for those few seconds in profile—delicate features, skin as pale as cotton, a mop of bright red hair. Chrysanthemums. Big, bushy blooms, vivid and teeming with innocence. And then the truck came.

Theo and Shauna arrived at a little after seven; Griff made martinis, which I noticed Shauna barely touched. I'd forgotten how beautiful she was. She had on a pair of jeans and a salmon-colored cashmere sweater. Her jewelry was big and bold and colorful. Her boots, adorable, and I told her so. She was in her last year at Columbia with a double major BA/BS in anthropology/biology. This, Griff and I already knew about her from my dad's party. I remember mentioning on our way home that night that she either has no idea what she wants to be or she has some grand plan. What we didn't know but learned over martinis: she had applied for and been accepted to Princeton to get her doctorate in geosciences. Apparently she had a grand plan. With palpable pride, Theo said, "Yeah, with her socio-cultural anthropology degree and the summer classes she's been taking at Cornell in natural resource management, she's going to, uh. You tell 'em, babe. You say it better."

"Theo, don't be an ass," Shauna said.

"No, tell us," Griff said. "It sounds interesting."

For the next ten minutes Shauna described her passions and plans while Griff and Theo peppered her with intelligent questions. Griff in particular seemed utterly captivated. All I could get was something about stakeholders and the need to understand their attitudes, beliefs, behaviors, and how doing so could advance the integration of human and ecological dimensions of natural resource management. "I'd like to approach my research through the integration of anthropology and ecology, utilizing the sub disciplines of social-ecological systems resilience theory and international relations theory."

That was when I gave up and drifted away—smiling in the right places, nodding assent—but my traitorous mind threaded its way back to the girl in the alley. I had this overwhelming desire to run screaming from our apartment, leave them to their highbrow discourse, and go look for this child who I had become certain must be in some sort of trouble. I was on my second martini when the conversation finally wound down. "Well," I said. "That's just fascinating. Congratulations, Shauna. Truly amazing. So. Shall we eat?"

Over dinner there were a lot of *wows* and *yums* and pleasantries.

"I'm extremely impressed," Shauna said. "This is absolutely fantastic. I wouldn't have the vaguest idea how to do gourmet."

"Nor should you," Theo said brightly. "What you're doing is much more important."

"Theo, please. You're being an ass again." Shauna said.

Without intending to I'm sure, my own brother had cut me off at the knees. Griff said nothing.

As soon as we all finished eating but before dessert, Theo stood and dinged his wine glass with his fork in a show of theatrics. Griff and I grinned at each other. We had expected something like this.

"Hear ye, hear ye," said my goofy brother. "I would like to announce to you and you only the engagement of Theo Tyminski and Shauna Russell."

Theo in fact is an actor. He has appeared in minor roles on Broadway and some significant roles off-Broadway. He and Shauna met when Shauna appeared backstage at one of his off-Broadway performances in which Theo had the lead, to congratulate her friend who had a very small role. Theo, seeing this gorgeous girl looking around, made a beeline to her side to flirt and fish for compliments. Shauna called him an ass, the friend introduced them, they'd been dating exclusively ever since.

Griff and I clapped and cheered and made our eyes big with surprise. The wedding would take place next spring. It would be held in Virginia where Shauna's family hailed.

Here was a beautiful, brilliant human being, nice, humble, a bit reserved—in a word, perfect. What in God's name did she see in my brother? But in fairness to Theo, he had just landed a supporting role in a major Broadway production; he'd had guest starring roles in a number of TV shows—maybe he was on his way. What did I know? They were both twenty-two, which I remembered as a year in a person's life filled with both grandiose hope and paralyzing horror. They seemed to have the hope part down, though neither exhibited the horror that I had experienced and to an extent still felt.

Other than Shauna's best friend, Griff and I were the only ones to know of their engagement.

"When are you gonna tell mom and dad?"

"Soon," Theo said. "Very soon, so don't you let any cat out of any bag—or I'll know who did it."

"Never," I said.

"Not us," Griff agreed.

After they left Griff cleaned up while I sat on the couch and finished off the bottle of wine. "Wow," he called from the kitchen. "Don't know how he did it, but your brother hit the jackpot."

I wanted to hate her but I recognized that my feelings had to do with self-loathing that I would have loved to redirect—my therapist would have been proud.

Griff and I made love that night, though honestly I was not really in the mood. It was nondescript, quiet. Afterward we kissed, said our I love yous. I stared at the ceiling and pictured the girl. I heard Mrs. Rayburn, the neighbor above us, walk to her bathroom; somewhere a cat yowled; a car sped by with music boiling from its windows; I heard the toilet flush; I heard Mrs. Rayburn's feet thump back across my ceiling. "Griff?" I whispered. "I saw a strange little girl with chrysanthemums in the alley by Ingrid's Market and um. Griff?" I rolled onto my side and watched my husband dream.

I was between careers. God, I hated that phrase. Griff was twenty-eight and I was twenty-six. My major in college had been philosophy. I'd had no grand plan. What I'd had was an abundance of confusion over what to do after graduation. I went to work at a Fortune 500 company in the finance sector, basically as a peon. For five years I scraped and scrambled and shoved my way to a middling position making six figures when I realized that my weekly $450 therapy sessions were centered on the debilitating anxieties of my job. One day my therapist, perhaps tired of hearing my ongoing diatribe, asked me if I'd considered quitting. Two hours later I considered it; the next day I quit. Griff, always supportive, generally easy-going, told me to take my time and find something that moved me, that made me feel alive. I didn't say it then, but I'll say it now: Griff sometimes surprised me how intuitive he could be—how he knew, before I'd ever put it into words, that I felt dead inside was beyond me.

I wasn't sleeping well. I found myself dreaming of the girl holding those chrysanthemums. Not every night, but enough that it began to bother me. You could say they were recurring dreams, though the venue was always different: an alley, a park, a busy street. The girl never changed. I saw her only from the side—delicate features, red hair, pale skin, chrysanthemums. In the dreams, just as I was about to see her face-on, I always woke up, sometimes with an echo of the bleating horn of a truck wanting to get by. Always I woke sweat-soaked, stinking, my hairline damp. By then Griff was up, dressed, gone for the day.

When I wasn't traipsing back and forth to Ingrid's, peering into that alley, scanning everyone on the street, buying things I didn't need—peaches, loaves of bread, toothpaste—I spent hours in our dark apartment agonizing over ideas for a career path. I went online; I looked at what other people were doing. Nothing was I even remotely qualified for. Worse, nothing appealed to me. Round and round I went; each evening, with a meekness that humiliated me, telling Griff, "Getting close."

One day my mother called. Apparently Theo and Shauna had given my parents the good news. I pretended I didn't know. We talked for a while about what kind of life they would have, being such different people. And then a pause in our conversation.

"So," my mom finally said. "Any ideas yet what you want to do?"

"Getting close," I said.

While she prattled on with annoying motherly advice, I gazed through our dining room window. Our apartment building had a small, fenced-in, community backyard. A patch of grass, a tree, small garden, bench. I half expected to see her hiding in the shadows with those taunting chrysanthemums. No one was there, just leaves blowing by in the wind.

"What about the chrysanthemums?" my therapist asked. "Any significance?"

I felt guilty paying out that kind of money for therapy after quitting my job. Griff, who had grown tired of hearing about some girl I saw in an alley, reminded me we had enough in savings. But still. "I don't know," I said. "They're not a flower I've ever thought much about."

"How about the red hair?"

I've known only a few people with red hair, most notably my great Aunt Bess, a sweet old lady who smelled remarkably like corn, but no one who ever caused me any pain or strife. "No," I said. "Nothing."

I'd told her about the dreams and predictably she encouraged me to crack them open, see if I could assign meaning to the scrambled images. At the end of the session, I was no closer to letting go of what seemed to be turning into an obsession. But it did mark the second time I saw the girl.

My mind is usually in a daze when I leave these sessions and unless the weather is inclement, I tend to like to walk the seventeen blocks home to gain some sort of composure before I have to see Griff. At a little after four I set out. The shadows were long, the air crisp with autumn. Red and copper leaves bounced along the sidewalks. People of all stripes floated past me in a blur. I'd forgotten my coat in the therapist's office and decided I didn't care.

Up ahead on the other side of the street a man operating a hot dog cart opened a drawer and a plume of steam rolled out. A woman in a red coat handed him money and took the hot dog. When she stepped away, my line of sight converged, a short distance beyond, on a lamppost and a tree. Between the two stood the girl with chrysanthemums. My heart knocked hard against my ribs; I couldn't breathe. She appeared as I'd first seen her in the alley, and dozens more times in the dead of night, in fevered dreams. This time I saw more of her face, though still at an angle. And I saw that her dress—the same slate gray as Griff's suit—was not a size too large but high yoked and loose, with gigot sleeves, the hem landing below her knees.

Heads bobbing, legs scissoring, torsos flickering by—on my side of the street and on hers—cut off and renewed my view of her in a strobe-like effect. I craned my neck, stood on my toes. "Move!" I shouted. "Move!" I plunged through bodies and sprinted into the street. The deafening sound of screeching tires melted into a lurid and momentary pain. Even as I knew I had left the ground and gone airborne, I kept my eyes on her. On those fat chrysanthemums; on her waxen skin; on those subtle features—her nose, her chin, her small red lips. On that mop of red hair covering her forehead, framing her cheeks.

Just as the pavement rose up to strike me her eyes found mine. They were large, beautiful eyes I remember, dark and round, like black marbles stitched into a doll's head. A haunting calmness I saw in those eyes—she could have been looking outward or inward, a thousand miles deep—and saw them glisten with pinprick starbursts of the setting sun before everything winked out.

I woke in darkness in a strange bed, a strange room; a sliver of fluorescent light spilled through a cracked door onto a wall. Next to the bar of light hung a clock. Too dark to read. A flat screen TV. A window with nothing but black sky and stars. Nothing made sense and I felt fear spidering through my veins. I opened my mouth to call out and a searing pain shot through my jaws, behind my ears, exploded at the top of my head. The door flew open; the light on the wall expanded and shrank; a dim light flicked on. An older woman in white pants and a colorful smock set her hand gently on my shoulder and told me not to talk, that I'd been in an accident, nothing that wouldn't heal. She began fiddling with a bag hanging on a post, with a long tube that emptied into my arm. Her voice soothed, even as her words began to blur and the space around her grew fuzzy. I was not surprised to see the girl standing in the corner clasping her chrysanthemums looking on.

Sometime over the next three days in that stark room with gray walls and linoleum floors and a window that bore the evolving sky—blue, twilight gray, black and starry, blue again—I was informed that I was a very lucky young lady. I'd broken my jaw and suffered a concussion. Contusions and abrasions snaked out over my entire body. Bandages were wrapped and removed and wrapped again. The bag that ended with a needle piercing my vein contained maximum pain killer, ample antibiotics and sufficient nutrition until I could suck on a straw. My jaws had been wired shut after the surgery and could stay that way for the next couple of months. Griff held my hand with such tenderness and said witnesses reported that I had darted out into the street, that the accident was my fault. I nodded. "Why?" he said. "What made you run out like that? Was someone threatening you?" The girl, clasping her chrysanthemums, stood quietly against the gray wall. Her calm, enigmatic visage lent me a kind of stoicism that served me well at the time. I averted my eyes.

On the third day Griff brought me home. The pain was manageable with the cocktail of drugs they gave me. My mother begged to come and stay with us. I begged Griff to say no. Consequently strangers showed up while Griff was at work, to see to my needs. He had helped exonerate another innocent who had been in prison for 27 years of a life sentence for a murder he didn't commit. I was deeply proud of Griff and at the same time unbearably envious. To have something so important, to do such good in the world—how do people find that? At times I wept with self-pity, which only added to my shame, and I wept all the more.

Theo showed up periodically, entertaining me with tales of rehearsals gone ridiculously wrong. My mother brought every kind of soup known to humankind and we established a kind of truce that both of us could abide. On weekends Theo brought Shauna whose kind and gracious demeanor made me ashamed of my earlier jealousy. But most days I spent alone in the dining room, reading or looking out the window at the community backyard, which no one inhabited but the girl with her chrysanthemums, who looked at me looking at her—sometimes for hours. Once I went to the window and pressed my face to the glass. But the moment I went out into the yard she was gone. I knew then our lives would be lived from afar.

Just before Halloween Therese my therapist stopped by and brought the coat I had left behind in her office that day. Because my jaw was wired shut, I'd cancelled our sessions for the foreseeable future. What was the point?

"Is that kale juice?" she asked.

The woman who was caring for me that day had shown Therese into the dining room where I sat gazing out the window, an open book on the table. I nodded yes and motioned to ask if she'd like one.

"No thanks. Much too healthy for an old bird like me." She smiled and looked at me intently. "Is she out there now?"

I nodded.

"That's what sent you into the street, wasn't it?"

I nodded again.

"Are you still dreaming of her?

Another nod.

She reached out and put her liver-spotted hand over mine. She had salt and pepper hair cut short and warm brown eyes. I truly liked her. I sensed her head turn to the window where a view of the backyard presented itself. "You know I can't see her, right? You know she's not real?"

It was a compound question. I averted my eyes.

One morning I went out to the backyard at sunrise and sat on the bench and waited. The girl with chrysanthemums never appeared. Eventually I looked over at the window of my dining room and there she was peering out at me as if we had exchanged places. I wanted to laugh. I was afraid to laugh, afraid of the pain. Something resembling laughter burbled up from my gut and escaped my lips without my jaw moving. Griff found me like that, burbling in the garden with the deadest expression on my face, and brought me in. The way he looked at me sent a chill up my spine.

We got through the holidays. At Thanksgiving I sucked on fragments of turkey until they disintegrated and slipped down my throat. By Christmas my jaw was set free and I was able to take bird-sized bites of ham and scalloped potatoes. I hummed while everyone sang carols. It still hurt to open my mouth; the vibration that comes with words spoken left me dizzy and frustrated. We exchanged gifts. I don't remember when I knew Griff was having an affair, but I remember quite well the day I didn't care.

On April 11, I gained a sister-in-law. The wedding, intimate and lovely. I liked her parents. They were small, gray-haired, warm. People whose arms you felt you could climb into and escape the world. None of us knew how they'd do—Shauna in school, Theo only weeks ago landing his first lead role on Broadway. Of one thing we were all quite certain: They didn't care. They were in love. Details would work themselves out.

Five days later, back from the wedding in Virginia—Griff doing great things, me floundering—I asked him to sit with me in the dining room. For the longest time my eyes settled on the window. Griff watched me carefully, perhaps knowing, perhaps not.

"I've filed for divorce," I said. "Probably you'll receive the papers sometime tomorrow. I'd like it if you could leave as soon as possible."

I thought he would say something. He said nothing. He took my hand in his, as tenderly as he always did, and wept.

I averted my eyes.

I still see her. In my dreams. In the world. I stopped my sessions with Therese or any therapist because I believed their ultimate goal would be to rid me of the girl and that's not something I desired.

On the day my divorce was final I met Griff for breakfast at a little café we both loved.

"You look great," he said.

"You too."

He told me all about his latest success and I congratulated him. This time with nothing but sincere admiration.

"I'd like it if we could have dinner now and then," he said. "I miss you."

"Maybe. Let's see."

"Well? So how's it going? Get anything figured out yet?"

"Getting close," I said.

Late in the month of August my dad came into my bedroom. The one I'd grown up in. The one I'd come crawling back to.

"Put some shoes on and get your purse!"

I was sitting on my bed with my sketch pad, drawing for the hundredth time the girl in her old-fashioned gray dress, her mop of red hair, her five big chrysanthemums. I had everything right—her small chin, petite nose, red expressionless lips. But the eyes. I could never quite get the eyes. Round. Black. Questioning maybe? Sad? Hopeful? Resigned? Expectant? I had seen those eyes a thousand times and they never changed; yet each time I looked at her, I felt something different. There were days when she'd stand in the corner of my room, oftentimes for hours, waiting for me to decipher whatever she meant me to know and get it onto my sketch pad.

"Why?" I mumbled. Theo got his goofiness from my dad. "Where are we going?"

I hadn't been to a carnival in years and going with my dad, even as a diversion, even as a way of trying to integrate myself back out into the world, was feverishly disorienting—the crowds, the noise, the nauseating smells of sugar and deep fry. Somewhere in the distance, the loud whistles of a calliope; barkers we passed demanding I step right up, knock over the cans, win a stuffed bear. And there she was, a child of such stark beauty, a wraith stuck in the tar pit of my mind. I saw her near the snack bar, the ticket booth, the carousel; she stood like a little talisman behind the clown who frightened me terribly with the gash of a big red grin, a bulbous nose, a balloon he forced into my hand.

I left my dad at the gate of a heart-bursting behemoth ride. I ran up the ramp, climbed aboard, watched the worker press go. He slung me about like a ragdoll, while the wind pulled my hair, battered my cheeks. I flew up up up and the sky crashed down. The world fractured into a million pieces, like a tornado of tiny découpages—surreal, varnished, intended. And who but me was the découpeur? A splash of gray dress. A dab of red hair. A swirl of white flowers. And that dreadful feeling that my chair would come loose and catapult me away to a hideous death—that's the fun; that's the horror. Now you're here. Now you're gone.

J. Condra Smith

Nork

Before the State of New York uprooted itself from the earth, back when the tremors felt more like vibrations from traffic than seismic events, what people first reported were the sounds: an unexplained buzz in the window panes, or at other times, a groan rising from the foundations of things. "Sonic phenomena." Hadn't someone on the news said that? Over the next several weeks, the vibrations intensified. Tremors became daily quakes. Months-long evacuations during this time let the natural world nose its way back over New York's cities in faint, ancestral recognition of the headwaters and swamps that once thrived there. Then came the massive upheavals of crust and sediment, when what seemed like the whole Northeastern United States reared up on its haunches. Now, with a final cataclysmic push, the State of New York wriggled free.

Emergency alerts didn't have a chance to hit the airwaves before New York was first spotted, lumbering south across morning traffic. Vacationing motorists mistook it for a geological landmark looming over a spree of northern Pennsylvania cedars—some unforeseen mountain range that had them scrambling for their guidebooks.

***

The elderly couple first saw it from the bedroom window, clear across their state. They thought it was a storm of apocalyptic proportions, just by the sheer mass of the thing, the way its silhouette obliterated the sun, the eastern sky. But there was something in its movements that resisted explanation, with its abrupt stops, the unexpected turns—and what to make of the twin columns at its base? How they worked in unison, scissoring leg-like over the terrain. It had the look of something they felt they should be able to recognize, but would never have thought possible enough to even guess. The look of something alive. Almost like this apocalyptic storm had been mapped onto a human silhouette.

Now the storm shifted to the south, just enough for the sun to break free. Its sudden light banished the silhouette across newly-revealed highlands, down through canyons and vertical planes. The storm was now gone. In its place, the couple found a colossal, moving landscape.

The revelation almost bowled them off their feet. Just on the other side of the window was the dawning of another world—a world with its own forests and bodies of water, which must have been preserved in a high-altitude freeze. There were even what looked like volcanic plumes rising from fissures in the world's chest and limbs. "Friction," came the consensus from radio reports. The couple was overtaken by a delirious feeling, like they were looking down at this landscape from high above, while at the same time watching it glide over them from far below. They couldn't move. Dueling forces of awe and terror kept them locked in that world's orbit, where they could neither yield to its gravity nor escape it. When they look back on this day, they'll feel how strange it was, and also how inevitable, that under New York's shadow they came together so readily after decades of strain.

For thirty-three years they'd shared the same home. Despite their confines, a distance had come between them. The space that once brought them physically close had unfolded into miles of tired familiarity. But beyond all that, the familiarity had been made ragged with grief.

For most of their adult lives, the couple had struggled to have a child. They had gone through a battery of sperm analyses, blood tests, hormone treatments. And all of this only to get knocked down by a false pregnancy years later, then the two early-term miscarriages. Still they persisted. By this point, the couple was old enough to take a dogged hope from the rituals of trying, while just young enough still to keep trying the rituals. For years they pushed on until everything else that connected them had fallen away. Little things that used to come together to make a life. There were the vinyl records they'd take turns waking each other up with each morning. And every year, they embarked on meticulously planned road trips, once even spending an entire month of saved vacation to ride the changing leaves north to south, like an autumnal wave down the east coast.

But fertility treatments tolled hard on their finances. Road trips became overnights at local bed-and-breakfasts, then petered out completely. They felt a distance growing between them. By now, they'd come to observe sex with joyless, routine frequency. Taking all these things' place at the center of their relationship was a kind of beleaguered hope. Then came the time when even this hope was worn down to the nib of its former self.

By the time the woman showed signs of a healthy pregnancy, the couple had sunk most of their savings towards an in-vitro procedure. They'd taken out a loan against their retirement and still had to mortgage their home. But now there would be this child, the woman thought to herself. Her body was creating a *child*.

It was suddenly clear that the sacrifices and even the wait had been part of its creation, making up the years of emotional labor that, in the agonizing thirst of it all, made its quenching that much sweeter. There was the false pregnancy to think about, but this time the changes coming over her were definite enough to cut through the fog of everything before, so that (she didn't know how else to explain it) she simply knew.

Once, an old friend of hers with two children said that every atom on earth— water, magma, the tissue of a human heart—came from a dying star. She said that after we die, she likes to believe our consciousness returns to the universe, like a second birth. And our bodies again become dead atoms. "But before that, we might bring a small part of that star back to life—by creating a baby."

This used to sound a little too flower-child for her taste. But here it was, actually happening inside her. She couldn't help but radiate with the thought that, right now, there were strands of ancient, cosmic matter weaving through her body to create new life. She began to feel connected to everyone, to everything around her: the man, complete strangers, the stars—the whole celestial scheme of things. It was like there were all of these fragments in her world, and joining them together now was this child.

In the months leading up to the birth, the woman would give weekly updates on its growth. "Baby's as big as a peppercorn!" she announced on week six. Just two weeks later, it had metamorphosed—miraculously—into a crustacean the size of an olive. "An olive. Can you imagine?" After the first trimester, the man lay his head on her belly and said, "How's it going in there, little Kiwi?" In the last three months of prenatal development alone, it grew three hundred times its previous size. Soon it would arrive as a perfect loaf of pumpernickel. Had it continued to grow at this rate, the couple wondered how big—how astronomically big—the child would be in ten years. In twenty.

Finally, the baby came to them gray and marbled in a pasty white film. It was a morning heavy with cloud cover, they remembered. Wet, gloppy snowfall made traffic to the hospital painfully slow. She began going into labor in the back seat of the car, twenty minutes out from the hospital. When they arrived, the woman was gurnied to the birthing suite.

Her labor lasted just under seven excruciating hours. When the baby came, something in the room's tone changed. The voices of the medical team became taught and subdued, and the couple realized the baby wasn't crying.

They watched, unable to move or breathe while their child lay on its own little table under a radiator. In the sharp light they could pick out small details: its brows, lightly penciled in, the delicately arranged porcelain of its toenails. Its fey nose with that upturned swoop. They watched the helpless form without blinking. It was theirs. For those few moments it was theirs and they were so in love, so completely undone.

Minutes later, the OBGYN removed the ventilator mask from the baby's face. He made a point not to look up until he sat down with the couple. He talked in a reverent near whisper, as if the baby left on the table were only sleeping. The couple nodded and cried soundlessly. Only later did they realize they hadn't heard, or didn't remember, what he'd said. When he left, the rest of the medical team gave the family time alone.

They took turns holding the baby with all the tender urgency that comes from trying to soak up a lifetime with their child in those moments, while knowing it was already too late. They pored over every feature of the baby's serene face, straining to get it all right in their memories.

The couple would never fully leave the birthing suite. Throughout their lives they'd carry it around with them, the whole ensconcing shell of it on their shoulders. When they returned home they found it was all they had left to share. They'd mentally rehearse the scene that had unfolded there—what they could remember of it, though they'd never be sure about the timeline of everything. Had the medical team really toweled their baby off before even placing the ventilator mask over its face? How long was it before the OBGYN called off attempts to resuscitate? The couple wondered if there was something they themselves had done wrong before the birth, or something they could have done better. They inhabited the space between these thoughts, each one leading into the next like a succession of walls, but without any door to exit through.

They stayed in the bereavement suite for two nights, and when they returned home, the man packed everything they'd prepared for the baby's homecoming. What he wanted, what he thought they both needed, was relief from their pain.

Sensory toys, diapers in bulk, onesies—he sorted and stored everything with an efficiency that grieved the woman. She didn't want to feel better. She didn't want to feel as if her baby had never happened. It was perverse thinking that way. Still, she wouldn't stop him. Whether she wanted relief or not, in some unacknowledged part of herself she was relieved, more and more with every load the man lugged off for donation. Of all the baby's things in the house, she reserved her protest for the crib. This they moved from the foot of their bed and into the guestroom.

A month later, the woman joined a volunteer program that created stuffed monkeys for children in the hospital. Almost overnight, the guest room became a craft studio, with the crib the only uncluttered space in the room. There were foldout tables, cubbies packed with supplies, and chairs for overflow.

Sometimes the man would awaken to find her asleep at her work table or curled up on the floor by the crib. He blinked at her for a full minute one night, unsure what was required of him. There had come a point early into the woman's labor when the pain carried her beyond the reach of anything he could say or do. It was as if she'd crossed some unseen threshold that he had no access to. He found her much the same way now as she was then—impossibly far away. Her pain untouchable. The helplessness frightened him at first until eventually, it wore him down. He began to take overtime at the lumber yard where he worked. The woman added new volunteer projects, in addition to her shifts at the drugstore. They secreted themselves into increasingly more remote corners of their grief, where over the next months and years they drifted apart with slow, tectonic force.

***

Today, evacuees log-jammed every major roadway on the eastern seaboard. The elderly couple was left with only their radio to take refuge in. If nothing else, the constant stream of information gave them the feeling of control. With New York taking up so much airspace, they found their television unreliable, a pixel storm of brightly-subtracted spaces. The radio wasn't much better, but its static gave an underlying calm to everything, like rain fizzing outside their window. And they were amazed to hear reports that New York drew a tide up the eastern shore of Lake Huron. The broadcasts sharpened their eyes to details too distant to make out on their own. They squinted until they saw how the sun's light conjured up floating bodies of water and once, what looked like a phantom city, drifting over the horizon of New York's stomach. The man could even see (he was sure) the mysterious fire-green auroras, which were said to be rippling through dust storms around New York's feet.

As morning turned to afternoon, the couple's fear became colored with wonder and later, even a sort of infatuation. One talk show host said, "We might have expected something like this from California, but New York?" They heard how this was the first landmass in recorded memory to do anything even remotely like this. It had peeled itself out of the earth's crust and the woman said, "How clever of it." There was a strange, unruly satisfaction at being won over by the same thing that struck them with so much uncertainty. All the grandeur and fear it stirred up before only made its unsteady gait so precious now. More than anything else, they were charmed by its humanness. How it toddled so becomingly. "Nyork," they named it. Then just, "Nork."

"Look at Nork!" the woman would say. And there it would be, shambling after thunderstorms, batting them into oblivion. When they learned that its leaking water table flushed out vast farmlands, they shook their heads wearily, saying, "Can you believe the mess?"

On-air that afternoon, a foreign zoologist said New York appeared to be growing more developed as the day progressed. The couple themselves noticed how articulate its movements seemed. But the explanation the zoologist gave surprised them. The more New York matured, she said, the smaller it became. Before sunset, just when Nork drew close enough for the couple to feel the thunder of its motion, they saw what was happening. With each footfall, debris came ballasting down Nork's body. County-sized hanks of Nork's face sheared away, while others hung grotesquely from some geologically inexplicable, fibrous matter. Even from hundreds of miles away, they could tell it was shrinking. Yet the zoologist had been right. A boost had come into its steps. It was as though Nork wasn't losing its body, so much as its burden. The couple imagined a small, humanlike essence at Nork's core. A sort of homunculus that was gradually shedding its husk. They could see its movements would continue to mature as its mass grew more and more human-sized. Maybe the satellites and surveillance drones that coordinated evacuations would lose track of it for a week. Then one day the lead story would be that New York was spotted in a trench coat, ducking into a diner on the Ohio border.

The first sign that something was wrong came with the late afternoon storms. Thunderheads, what looked like a phalanx of them, climbed out of the distant hills, while others grew around Nork's feet, like they'd extracted themselves out of the dust clouds. Lightning slung across its path in brief, plasmatic webs. Sudden downpours accelerated the erosion of Nork's body. It stumbled, then pitched headlong to the earth. The storms took liberties with Nork's limbs as it crawled forward. It was then on what must have been its hands and knees that Nork gave up a cry that rang through the couple's windows and threatened the ceramics on their shelves.

The man couldn't bring himself to look. "We should go," he said. The woman wouldn't move. Every cell inside her swelled towards Nork's struggling figure. She seized with longing to do—something. Anything. But all she could do was open the window and lean out. The cry grew more piercing. Lightbulbs went off with a pop. "Come on," the man said. He tried coaxing her back in. He reached to close the window, but she held back his hands. They looked on wordlessly while they moved toward each other.

There was something like yearning in their touch, but also pain. It was like they were reaching across years of solitude to find that their parts no longer fit. Still they moved closer, insisting themselves against the incongruous curves of their bodies. A sense of release welled up; emotions they'd kept to themselves for years now moved freely between them.

A sudden wind shook the neighboring wheat fields. Airborne particles ticked the window. The couple turned to look. Dusk was beginning to fall, but through the window they could discern the cloud cover splitting apart. Then through the storm canopy's center, there was Nork, lifting itself waveringly to its feet.

A cheer caught in the man's throat. The couple held each other close and watched. There was a weightlessness now that seemed to be at work over Nork's body. It looked like what it had lost in mass, it gained in buoyancy.

Already Nork stood higher in its smaller form than it ever had at its most massive, yet still it continued to straighten—up through the atmospheric layers, throwing weather systems into disarray until the sky around it had almost completely cleared. From the radio, the couple learned that satellites were filming as Nork's head approached the thermosphere, where it had just started to crown. They looked up.

There, Nork stood like a bridge to the sky: with the moon now fully eclipsed, the darkness of space rinsed over Nork's shoulders and down its back. Stars awoke, bleary in the early night. Manhattan became suddenly luminous, with what looked like the whole cosmos snared in its spires. It was Queens, though, and the Bronx that first caught the light that the sun directed towards the moon. One by one, the city's boroughs became so fully incandescent that the rest of the state seemed blanked out by comparison, until all the couple could see was this lunar city sailing up to meet the stars.

"Isn't it miraculous?" the woman said.

Now, the vacuum of space caught Nork's upper body so that its debris began cascading in reverse. Both the woman and the man felt a tweak in their joints as Nork pulled gradually apart at the elbows. They wondered quietly, too horrified to ask aloud, if Nork might soon disintegrate to nothing. Yet as the minutes passed, they saw that it was escaping the Earth in a bound—vaulting, vaulting into the distance, until it took up no more space against the sky than an olive, a peppercorn, then nothing at all.

Marc Levy

Larosa Dreaming

"When harvest time arrives, the farmer must first approve the luster and subtle coloring in the fruits of his labors. Then he must approach each vegetable in turn, starting with the carrot. He squats down, reaches out and plucks the first allurement from its dark narrow passageway in the moist earth. He drenches the dirt away by dipping it into his aluminum watering can, then shushing it around. Then he resurrects the carrot from its cool bath. He bites the tip off and spits it away. Oh, the glorious taste!, as he partakes of its orangey ripe toughness. Thus do he and the carrot perform that healthy crunch, which is audible among all other growths.

"There is nothing like this: the first fruit! The farmer deserves it. It is the spring ritual. It is sacramental and is true also of flowers and the weaning of harvested dogs."

This is how it happened. Larosa made a list, then sent out invitations. Everyone responded. Catty Plowgirl was the first, arriving with her romantic farming tale. She wore a dress made of flower sacks and a floppy straw hat. Then came Count Bellicose in a tattered purple cape draped carelessly over his shoulders, above which his bowling ball head wobbled, and his grim smile, designed to control all situations, was fixed, it seemed permanently, in place.

The four others arrived, one by one: Coach Wannabe, Eleanora Crestfallen, Hans Hammerschmidt, that fixture at the nudist camp, naked under his tuxedo, and Gerald Cumquat, the fruit and vegetable tosser.

And then there was, of course, Larosa herself, named for the great Italian Baritone, Julius La Rosa, who had the voice of an angel and left it behind in Crivitz Wisconsin, where Larosa's grandfather took her fishing when she was a small child born into a Portugese American family. She was still a small child, yet dressed for the party in an elegant mauve pantsuit, appropriate to her station as the manager of the fine, six story department store downtown.

Things proceeded without a hitch. Hamburgies and hot dogs, Cheetos and Cool Aid, and jujubes and chocolate chip cookies for desert.

The Count gobbled with his mouth open. Catty searched for vegetables, especially carrots. Crestfallen munched at the tip of a hot dog while thinking of all lost opportunities, and the others traded success stories and insults when they were caught out. And Larosa mingled, sure of herself, staring pointedly into the eyes of the unsuccessful, those whose dreams of the future had betrayed them.

"When the sun rises," Catty said, "Certain viewers believe (deep down) that they have caused it to rise. These are few in number, and their source seems to be the story of the native who goes to the shore of the river, beats his drum, and the sun rises. Farmers, aware of nature and the galaxies, do not believe this. To believe this one must be a sure footed aristocrat."

"Nonsense!" Count Bellicose proclaimed while ducking a grapefruit thrown at his head by Cumquat. "We of the higher classes are not beguiled."

"Yeah, sure." Hans rejoined, shifting his naked belly under his scratchy cummerbund. "You ain't really a Count at all. Just a faker who works at the stock yards shoveling shit."

"My dear man," the Count responded. "I..."

"Betrayed us!" It was Eleanora Crestfallen. "Some boss you were. We were supposed to go places, to succeed. Look at us now. Nothing! Maybe this was in us all along. Betrayer!"

"*Scheissekopf!*" Growled Hammerschmidt, as Cumquat's ripe tomato banged into the Count's shoulder, soaking it's red juice into his cape. Crestfallen wept.

Thus it developed, this gathering in a future. And there was music, those pop tunes vaguely remembered from the common past. "Earth Angel," "Shu Boom Shu Boom," the ironic "Rags to Riches." And finally, in the present, "Send in the Clowns," whereby all garments fell away, those wished for coverings, leaving the guests in their naked realities.

All this was Larosa, wide awake and dreaming. She had made drawings and colored them in. Billy the Bully had become Bellicose. Catty was Barbie Lang. And, though peripheral, yet taunting, the three others had their place, the whole of this place and it's "children" gathered for The End of Days.

Sister Mary Polanski had told them a tale. "You must not bite down on the host after your receive it in your mouth after communion. There was a boy who spat the host into his handkerchief and took it home. Then, alone in his room, he unknowingly blasphemed. He lifted the host from his handkerchief, eyed it with derision, and bit into it.

"Immediately, the blood of Christ squirted out, striking him in both eyes. This boy who had violated the body and blood of the Savior, was blinded by it. He never saw a single thing again.

"The lesson is clear."

The next day, in the playground, the lesson arrived. They had her against the wall, and though she cried and screamed for her mother, she was pelted with raspberry soda; ripe tomatoes were thrown; stale potato chips rained down on her. And Billy the Bully led the charge, with Catty right beside him and the others fanned out around them, each engaged in the brutal defilement of the seven year old Larosa.

And after the Easter bombardment, cheap candied eggs, real eggs, and the proverbial sprays from soda bottles and squirt guns, Larosa began to fashion her plan.

How could a seven year old see so far ahead?

The temporary Band Stand would be fourteen feet high and constructed above the cement turn around to the side of the entrance into the school. It would be used for all manner of events: Glee Club, spelling contests, Drama Club presentations, Choir, and more.

It was this last item that interested her. The choir was small and all of her tormenters were in it. There might be collateral damage, but maybe not.

As the bombardments continued, Larosa studied termites and cellulose insulation. "The books say termites take around five months to eat through a foot long section of two-by-for, and they eat even quicker when confronted with cellulose."

The Band Stand stood above two-by-sixes. "Figure about a month to eat enough so that I can get the saw into a dissolving grove. Once it begins to fall, I'll skip to the wall against which it's anchored. I'll be safe back there."

Billy the bully had a plan. They would take her into the woods beyond the school grounds and depants her. Then they'd hang her dirty under ware on the flagpole beside the school's entrance. If her under pants weren't dirty, they would soil them good before hanging them. Barbie Lang would take care of this part.

Meanwhile, Larosa gathered her termites and the cellulose insulation she managed to pull from a crack in the finished basement wall of her home. Once the platform was up and finished, she took her termites and insulation, wrapped the latter around the two-by-six, and let the miniature beasts have at it.

She fought them off as best she could, but they accomplished their evil task, scratching and pawing her in the bargain She didn't weep or cry out. She fixed her mind on the Band Stand and the future, even when they were finished and were pointing out her dirty garment to any student who happened to pass by, and this included most everyone since the flag pole was close by the school's entrance.

Then came the beautiful day. The choir was singing some insipid religious tune, one issuing in those Christian pop song groups of the sixties. And Larosa was down below them, her sawing a dissonant, sad accompaniment to their straining voices.

As the bandstand began to fall and Larosa skipped to safety, yells and screams could be heard even from her hiding place. She was pleased with the sounds. Billy the Bully was killed and so was Barbie. Georgie and Sissy were severely injured. Nathan had a broken arm, and Toughie escaped unscathed, though he suffered for many years from traumatic stress disorder.

Ah, but once again, all this has been Larosa dreaming. No Band Stand, no saw or termites. Only the six were real, and they continued their harassments up until the day when the nuns, led by Sister Polanski and her ruler, doled out corporal punishment, rendering the crew temporarily incapacitated, while Larosa's only retribution was to escape.

Her family moved to a different school district. Billy the Bully, Barbie and the rest were left behind, chastised, yet in search of another victim.

Third grade proved to be a dream! *Vivo Sonhando*!

Michelle DeLong

Dreaming of J. Peterman

<u>Brooklyn</u>.

2 am, Bushwick.

You haven't eaten anything all day aside from spoonfuls of peanut butter straight out of the jar, and you're ravenously hungry. Too broke or cheap or both to justify the Postmates delivery fee, you reach for your worst grey outfit and set off bravely for the corner store.

As you contemplate mozzarella cheese sticks, you spot him: an off-the-market ex-fling wearing a three-piece suit. He is alone and carries an aura of recent emotional damage, the type that lowers one's inhibitions.

Flirtation and an ensuing moral dilemma won't be necessary–all grey everything is the moment, and the moment is *starving, cramping, on deadline, never been less horny.*

100% percale cotton sweat suit in a timeless heathered grey, absolutely shapeless, elastic banded, tapered in a way that suggests intentional celibacy and bodega meat pies enjoyed alone, hunched over the trash can, probably.

Price: $89

<u>Barcelona</u>.

2016.

Pandemic? Never heard of her. It's Friday night in Catalonia, naturally, and you're craving the hands, sweat, and hot breath of absolute strangers.

Friendly cab driver kisses both cheeks and pays you a compliment. Club Opium, a pile of coke snorted off the toilet seat with a girl you met in line for the restroom. Sunrise, your come-fuck-me heels strewn on the sand beside you, a drag from the bartender's cigarette–delicious.

8 a.m. train bound for Verdaguer, barefoot and still buzzing, heels in hand. An older woman in a business suit touches your face and tells you you're beautiful. You pop into the Sagrada Familia on a lark, where throngs of people push and push. You reach your arms out, ready to receive them.

Patent leather strappy stilettos in Gothic Quarter at Midnight, Gaudi Gold-trimmed Ocean, Raval Sex Worker Red, and Pot Brownie at the Dalí Museum Multicolor.

Price: $229.

Nancy J. Fagan

Love in the Time of Tumor

I don't think anyone can prepare themselves for the news that they have a brain tumor.

Glioblastoma. I am not sure if that's the exact kind or if it's merely a general category of the type of tumor that I had. What I learned is that it is a tumor which takes many things away, like verbal expression and upright ambulation, though no one mentioned what it does to undying love. It made my right arm relatively useless and that is concerning as I am an artist of some note, who is right-handed. In the process of building a show for *Paris*, headaches thundered into my life. Paris. Ten years out of art school, I quit my job at the deli and, at the age of thirty-four, could finally say with certitude, "I am an artist." I wondered if there were modifications to the term when one could no longer hold a paintbrush.

Fresh from our honeymoon, I reached into the soft microfiber couch to fetch the remote and, instead, suffered an astounding nausea that sent me spinning in all directions. Pain sheared through my brain with an abruptness that caused me to crumple to the floor. I could not escape it with ice or Motrin or even by thumping my head with my palm. I thought I had an ear infection or a migraine or anything but a glioblastoma. Suddenly, my words jumbled as if trapped in a web, and I could not say what I meant. I felt useless, empty, incapable. The headaches eased as the day ended, though I'm not sure any doctor understood why. If they've explained it to me, either I've forgotten, else the tumor got in the way of the information. It's all about pathways, it's all about interruption.

The first MRI sent shudders of clanging magnetic waves that bounced off that clump of cells. I felt a tingle through my spinal cord. Face up in the machine, they tucked me under a warmed blanket, a flurry of music in my headphones barely audible against the clatter. A kind man spoke in soothing tones with a Jamaican-laced accent, populating words around the noise.

"How are you feeling, Mrs. Lizana?" he asked.

I imagined that he gauged the fear in my eyes as he examined me through the machine's camera.

"Don't move now, just five more minutes for this view," he said. He had an authority that I could not defy so I froze in the helmet that held me there.

"Count to twenty for me," he said before more clanging and rat-a-tat-tatting. He turned the music off, I think. "Move your toes. Open and close your left hand. Do the same on the right."

He must have seen my mouth tighten.

"At least try."

When the noises stopped, a sense of dread washed over me.

"You did great," he said and moved me out of the machine by way of a conveyer belt that hissed itself open. I teetered slightly as I stood, so he steadied me. His scent drew me closer—Irish Spring soap, a deep breath of freshness. He looked up when I met his eyes. There it is, I thought. *He knows.*

The doctor, a friendly stranger, led me to a compact office to the left of the MRI room. It seemed easier for me to walk left.

"We'll need some more tests, we'll refer you to an oncologist, a specialist," he said gently. "You have to go to the hospital tonight."

"I have things to do," I replied, though I was simply not sure what.

He looked at Matteo. "The tumor will affect her thinking, may even affect her language or how she sees you."

"Her vision?" Matteo asked.

"No, her feelings. They may be upended. She'll likely be confused." He rubbed his hands together. "Hallucinations are not uncommon."

"Home," I said, and rose from the chair.

The doctor's voice was low. "This is more important."

"My favorite pajamas." I tried to argue but my words twisted, so I sat down and puzzled my thoughts as they spiraled around the tumor.

Matteo snugged his chair close to me and held my left hand soundly with both of his, our wedding bands shiny under the fluorescent lights. As the doctor explained where Matteo should take me next, I looked around the box of an office. There was a diploma in a black frame behind the doctor's blonde head and I cocked my own head to read it. The letters seemed like they were written backwards or upside down. It was either Latin or some secret Cyrillic script.

"It will be okay, Bella," Matteo said.

"Sure, I'm sure," I replied, though I was not sure of anything at all.

I blinked at Matteo, and examined his dark hair, goatee, and John Lennon glasses. He loomed over me, an umbrella over my frailness. I put my hand to my mouth and felt my lips skew to one side.

"We can't plan more until we have the tests back," continued the doctor. "But this is a marathon, not a sprint. You should know that."

Though his eyes focused on me, I turned away. My brand-new husband stroked my thigh with two fingers, an absentminded gesture I usually took to mean he was horny. I shook my head and tried to think. Did he really want to do it right there, in front of the doctor?

"Now?" I said looking from the doctor to Matteo. "Here, now?" I laughed wildly.

"Do what?" he asked. He bit his lower lip and his face paled.

"Get to it," I nodded at the doctor and knew he'd understand.

The doctor cleared his throat. "Sometimes patients experience unusual feelings that don't make sense." He hesitated. "Inappropriate. Like this."

I moved my hand to pull myself closer to Matteo, to touch him, to stroke him. But my right arm flopped off the edge of the chair and dragged me with it. The doctor leapt from his seat and the two strong men, one Italian and one Scandinavian, hoisted me up as if sharing a trophy. *They both want me.* I smiled at the potency of my glioblastoma. I was giddy all the way home.

"Why are you laughing?" Matteo asked as he drove into our driveway.

"I can, it's all mine," I replied. I pulled him inside the house.

He stood in the doorway of our bedroom.

"Are you sure?" he asked. "It feels wrong."

"Oh, yes." I smiled at him and reached for his belt.

Day one ended with intense lovemaking, the kind of love you make when you believe one of you will die soon, or as if you are under sniper fire, or lost at sea. I imagined all three.

Day two brought a host of people; another doctor, a nurse practitioner, another nurse, and a toothy receptionist who assured me that they were there to help me, that my health was the most important thing, then checked with my insurance before making any appointments. Scans, biopsy, surgery, chemotherapy, radiation, surgery again. The to-do list for a glioblastoma is long and involves a roomful.

Matteo and I were stunned at my rapid descent into feebleness. He led me by the hand when we took a walk and steadied me as I weaved from side to side. We tried to watch Netflix and play backgammon, but the actors and the checkers kept switching places. He sang to me, and the voice I once thought was lovely now grated on my eardrum like rough wool. He helped me do the most personal of things until I was profoundly humbled.

"I don't mind," Matteo insisted, running my hair through swirls of warm water over the bathroom sink.

"No, it's not good," I tried to explain, and pushed a box of tampons away with my foot.

"When you're better, we'll be okay," he said. "I'm here, I'll be here."

He wiped a tear from my cheek.

The first month blurred as days melted into weeks. I was able to dress, though sometimes I missed a few buttons. As my energy waned, Matteo chauffeured me and cooked for me and coddled me. He started a routine.

"Bella, I'll make all the meals, I'll do the laundry every Thursday," he added.

I'd catch him staring, as if he was trying to engrave my profile in his normal brain. Sometimes he actually drew me when I was exercising my nearly useless right hand. I stared at my image, captured on his page, and noticed the curious smile. He worked it with tiny hatch marks in the corners, then blended the pencil to soften the overall effect.

"Put the tumor right there." I pointed at a spot just above my left ear.

"Bella, no." He folded his pad closed.

He once tried to market his drawings. They were deeply saturated with color and hinted at violence. This was not the art that his culture generally appreciated, and he came to the United States with a hope that was flushed out of him quickly. He worked as a truck driver instead. When he came home at night, he tried to keep our life together alive for me.

He showed me our honeymoon pictures.

"Look, here's the night we went to Da I Gemelli." He pointed at my image, a plate of fried squid in front of me against a backdrop of the sea. The harbor was dotted with small colorful rowboats, floating against their moorings. I looked relaxed and sated. The next photo was of him, a salty olive between his teeth, grinning at me. Our trip was recorded in the photos but most of it was lost from my memory.

I knew the facts; we biked through Italy, weaving in and around the streets of his hometown. We drank wine and dipped hunks of homemade bread in glistening olive oil. We ate hearty Tuscan meals of beans and fresh vegetables and watched the sun set into the Mediterranean. But I did not actually remember it. He tried to help me.

"You said, 'We should come here every year'." He looked at me earnestly.

"Maybe." I had no memory of wanting that. I did not want that.

A guidebook on cycling through Europe, unpacked but not put away, was on the coffee table and I pushed it to the floor. Each day I was reminded of something I could no longer do. I tried to read an email offer from the discount ticket site. I gathered up the words I could catch and pointed at the laptop.

"Broadway, deli sandwich?" I turned in the direction of the train station. Nothing came out right anymore.

"Not yet, Bella, but soon," he said. "Let's wait until they take it out. Your tumor. We'll celebrate."

It was *my* tumor, not *the* tumor or *a* tumor. Mine, alone. The surgeries seemed to repeat. One to biopsy, one to remove, one to map. Then again. Seizures came and went, and I slept deeply in between. Matteo placed a calendar on the counter and crossed off each day's appointments. Once a week, while I stared at him from the couch, he spread my medicine bottles across the kitchen table and dropped pills one by one into the blue CVS pill organizer. He washed the glass on top of the table with vinegar after he was finished, taking care not to leave any traces of poison.

"Different from before," I said.

"Yes, Bella, it is." His sable eyes shined. "I love you."

"Yes, you do." I knew I could hurt him, so I said what was kindest.

My parents visited; their faces solemn as I smiled the hour away. My friends came in and out through a haze of coffee cake and crockpot meals. Words also came and went so the visits were disjointed with conversation between them instead of with me. I stayed where they put me, I ate when I was told to, and I tried a number of times to exercise my right arm. The physical therapist crooked my fingers around a paintbrush and moved my arm in elementary shapes to produce a lopsided triangle or skewed oval.

Sometimes, I could form an okay sign with the hand, my fingers meeting in an O, and we celebrated.

"You did it," she said.

"Tried," I replied and wiggled my fingers around to form 'okay' again.

My best friend Tina, a nurse, gestured to her medical journals on the coffee table. She pointed to photos and diagrams of the medicines I was forced to take. She explained the side effects, "anorexia, vomiting, fatigue," as if they were desirable.

"That means the chemo is working," she said, her eyes filled with fervor. "You can beat this." She told me to visualize the medicine as it worked.

Everyone, simply everyone, asked me, "What can I do to help?" and I smiled and said, "I'm good." They could never give me back what I needed. My feelings, my former self.

I stared at the pile of thank you cards left unfinished, and the few wedding gifts stacked in the corner covered in silver and gold paper. I had no idea how long ago our ceremony had taken place, with time sliding off into an abyss, but the presence of these things filled me with unease. One day I tossed a blanket over them and they disappeared the next morning.

"I'll take care of the presents," Matteo said. "I'll write the notes." Bags were strung under his eyes and the worry lines near his temples grew deeper each day.

My ring fell off in September, when my body withered just enough. Matteo hung the diamond-studded band on a sturdy cord around my neck.

"It's better here, close to your heart," he said, while stroking my chest with his calloused hand.

"Put the damn thing away." When words came, they were sharp.

He shook his head.

One day, in the cool light of late autumn, I thought of something and waved to him as I organized the words.

"Do you want some soup?" Matteo asked. He held a bowl of tomato broth.

"I want to paint," I told him, straining to emphasize the word paint.

He wheeled me to a corner of the bedroom, to an easel that he lowered to match my wheelchair's height and readied a palette of colors for me. I looked at the blank canvas and studied the small dots ingrained in its weave. I watched quietly as they swirled into a pattern that burst into a blue flame. I held the brush in my left hand, closed my right eye, and tried to paint straight lines through the fire, but the brush wriggled and my lines wilted to an ember. I tried again and failed. *Paris*, I thought. I tipped the palette to the floor and watched the globs of paint dribble across the hardwood. Matteo stood silently in the doorway watching.

Steroids kept me alert at two a.m. While the neighborhood crawled with vermin and stray cats, my skin prickled and buzzed with fever. Each night, I propped myself on an elbow and watched Matteo's mouth flutter as he snored like a dog. *He's so alive*, I thought. And I'm disturbed.

When I closed my eyes, I saw vibrant displays of the chemical compositional structure of the drugs Tina told me about that hummed through my veins every other week. Atomic numbers twirled around their scaffolding and created Venn diagrams of color and light. I imagined the vasculature of my corneas. I could see the chemotherapeutic agents whiz up and down in precise circles and flow through each vessel, flowering into lopsided balloons of translucency. One night, I smelled the acrid scent of sulfur as my blood brain barrier was breached. I pressed my fingers against blazes of light that Spirographed into moments of lucidness. My thoughts stunned me.

It's time to leave him. Paris is waiting. If I could get myself there, things would be better, I could start my life anew. Matteo snorted and I turned on my side, the one where the tumor once lived, to feel it inside me again, examine its hole. When I imagined my fingers exploring the cavern, I saw her for the first time.

She was a finely boned lady with porcelain skin who stood fourteen inches tall, roller skating and waving before dancing back into the spin art of my dream. She carried a paisley tote bag that I assumed was filled with schoolbooks, as her hair was tucked into a teacher's chestnut bun. Every day, thereafter, I saw her in the same outfit—black pedal pusher pants with a blush floral top, a white sweater tied neatly over her shoulders. She smelled like the hyacinths on her shirt. Freud would say that this vision was a manifestation of some repressed sexual urge, but I had no sexual yearnings, none, anymore. I think she symbolized something far more important, and I kept trying to reach her to figure it out, but I always stirred at the brink of discovery which whisked her away. I kept her hidden, deep within my dreams, so no one could take her from me.

One afternoon, in between treatments, I sat on the front patio and counted the cars that drove past.

"Bella, do you want to try a walk?" Matteo offered. He was full of questions.

I'd overheard Tina remind him that my tumor might interrupt normal feelings so he shouldn't be offended if I said something rude. He offered me all sorts of things, determined as he was to meet my needs. Food, hygiene, ambulation. He wanted to read to me, like he did on the beach in the Mediterranean, without the sex that followed. One day, he asked if I still loved him.

"Not so," I said. Frankly, I was over Matteo. The tumor absorbed the love we shared and when it was removed, there my feelings went. I didn't want the love back; I wanted to sit on my porch alone, count the cars, and dream of Paris.

That afternoon, ignoring Matteo and his questions, I felt a strange yawing behind my eye. I held my breath and tuned my ear to listen to the tumor-hole's blood that pulsated like the snap and crackle of cellophane. I felt something squeeze tight inside my skull and followed the sensation down a bumpy corridor through my brain. With a little flurry of snaps, like the applause for a poet, she squeaked slowly out of my ear and skated by for the first time in broad daylight. I laughed wildly and Matteo patted my arm, not bothering to look my way. She held her roll for a moment, turned towards me, and her face swelled my heart.

"Look, she's there," I said and pointed at the road.

"Yes, you're here," Matteo reassured himself.

The finely boned lady and I became great friends as more tumors were born from the site of the first. Though they ebbed with treatment, they bloomed again with fury. All the while, the lady peeked around MRI machines and PET scanners. She stood outside the drug store and watched Matteo go inside for medicine and, once, for a bag of salt and vinegar chips because it was all I could eat that day. I murmured to her and Matteo asked, "What did you say?" so I smiled at him and pointed at the air she lived in.

"I love her."

"I love you too Bella," he said, choking on the words.

The poor man still loved me.

The doctor watched me touch my head with my left pointer.

"Noise, sizzle," I said, my eyes open as wide as possible.

"You're doing just fine," he said and patted my dead arm.

Why does everyone pat me? The whole idea of it made me giggle.

One surgery was performed while I was wide awake. Awake with my brain open to the air. I felt it, in a way, like a whiff of fresh lilac across my ventricles, those small basins in my brain.

"I want you to sing Row, Row, Row, Your Boat," the doctor said.

"Your milk lasagna," I sang on key.

"Good, very good," he answered.

I wondered what he had for breakfast, what gave him the musty smell of a wet toad. I sensed it through my open skull, somehow bypassing all the usual connections. Suddenly, I realized what would cure me as a sense of clarity ticked through my synapses. At the moment of discovery, I tried to speak, to tell him and the others in the room the answer, but then he touched a spot that made me turn black inside and all the color drained from my thought. I heard his voice, distant, above the slurp of the suction machine, the whir of the IV apparatus, and the whispered zippity-zap of the cautery.

"That's the last one, I think we got all the new tumors," he said.

This, I understood.

My lady, Milady, was there too, in the corner. She seemed worried because she kept tying and untying her skates. I reached for the royal blue laces to help, but then they strapped my hand down on the table with a big run of Velcro. I smelled something burning, heard a crunch, then my nose drowned under the odor of disinfectant. I sincerely hoped they would not pour it inside my skull, though I could not stop them.

"Count down from twenty," the doctor said.

I smiled and imagined his bifocals and the black of his pupils.

"Seven eight nine," I said and laughed until my body shook beneath the drapes.

Milady winked at me, an impish grin on her face. She tied her skates and scooted out.

Matteo waited in my room; his routine disrupted routinely now. He wiped my brow with a coarse washcloth. It felt warm and dangerous. He held a mirror so I could adjust my bandage though I reached past it and moved the pillow instead.

"Sto bene," I said, smiling at him. "I'm fine." Sometimes things came out just right.

He kissed my cheek, put my right arm back up on the bed, and I laughed again.

Six months of failed medicines left me with a fair sense of what was coming. I'd hear the doctors and Matteo talk about experiments they might do on me. Gene splicing, new drugs that caused heart failure, and lobotomies. They talked about comfort, they talked about keeping me free from pain. Then they'd ask my opinion and I'd smile, the one thing I could manage to do beside count. The few words I had at this point were single phrases like 'want milk,' 'drink soup,' and the big one, 'more lasagna.' I smiled my way through lumbar punctures and biopsies. I smiled my way through long bouts of vomiting. Tina told me I even smiled during seizures.

He took a leave from work to be with me until the end. He rubbed my back and stroked my thigh, but it meant something entirely different now. It meant goodbye. I have to say, I didn't care much either way. There was little pain; the headaches had disappeared. I could still hear an echo in the hole my big tumor left, and the whistling through of my blood, so they gave me morphine to help me at night which dragged me through sleep.

When I came to the end, my fingers were so cold I could not point or tell Matteo milk, soup, or lasagna any longer. He and Tina watched me, turned me, wiped me. My parents kept up their vigil from the shadow of the hospital room. The doctor asked if I wanted to try one last thing. I shook myself hard, attempted to sit up to tell him no. Milady waited on the corner of my blanket.

Instead, I said, "Choose."

Matteo considered this, then turned to the doctor.

"Do everything," he said, his eyes bright with tears.

The hissing was constant, a machine pulsed with the rhythm of my heartbeat, and another squeezed my arm repeatedly. Milady stayed on the bed and waved in the nurses' faces. She wore patent leather pumps now, her roller-skating days behind us. She crossed her legs in pin-up style and let her hair stream out of the bun. She cooed to me and told me about her students.

"Prescott and Frank are the troublemakers," she said.

I could not answer her, nor smile. Everything was gone.

She understood my thoughts and we passed the time together like we shared a soul.

When Tina came to visit, she murmured to the doctors and read me poetry in French.

"Dans ce temps là, la vie était plus belle," she said, reading from a book by Prévert.

I tried to translate in my head, something about a time when life was beautiful. Tina didn't know the beauty and the vibrance of the world that I saw every day and how sweet it was behind my eyelids. Better than this life, much better with Milady.

We came home so Matteo could pay the bills and I could die. I shuffled through the small apartment picking up books or a vase and moving them to a different spot. Matteo walked behind me until I needed him to carry me to a chair or the couch. My arms and legs were the size of sticks and my cheeks sunk so deep within my skull I could hear them. They'd cut my hair so he could comb it easily, though the curls stuck soundly together.

"You're so beautiful," he said, stroking the bones of my face.

"So. So." I said, feeling my mouth sag to a trickle of drool.

One day, I dozed on the couch and awoke with a start.

"My pad," I said.

His eyes shifted quickly.

"Your sketchpad?"

"Mine." I said.

"Bella, you can't do it, just sleep," he murmured, stroking my thigh with two fingers.

"My pad." I felt my lips churn into a thin line.

"Okay, then." He waited for me to say more, but instead I glared.

He dug through the closet. He pulled out the still unwrapped wedding gifts and the unwritten thank you cards first, then he found my pad. He sat on the couch next to me, his weariness apparent as he handed me the pencil.

I held it in my left hand, and it vibrated as I touched it to the paper. I started at the top and began to draw what I saw behind my eyelids—the spindly webs of electric light that burned through. I drew for an hour as he sat next to me, his mouth hanging open. Milady sat on the coffee table and peered over the wire coil at the top of the pad.

"Nice," she said. Her lips shined as if painted with lemon zest.

I dropped the pencil twice and Matteo snatched it up and placed it back in my hand. He sat erect; his mouth froze to an o. Again, I drew. I shaded and hatched and x'ed out some contours. I did this every day. On day three, he called the doctor.

"I think it worked," he said, a note of caution in his voice. "She actually sits and draws now. She's getting stronger."

He hung up the phone and told me that I needed to go for another test, this one a special type of scanner that would tell us if the treatment worked. I smiled.

The machine ran back and forth over my head. I didn't hear much of anything. I searched my eyelids for a zing of light or a speckled pattern but only saw grey. Milady sat near my right hand and looked directly at me. I sensed her worry. Suddenly, she swirled into a point of light and dissolved through a pinhole in space.

We came home and Matteo smiled the way I used to. He made lasagna and soup for me, content to watch me feed myself with my left hand. I sat on the patio, surveying the street, aware of his ever-present grin. I searched the insides of my eyelids all day and night, but I could not find her anywhere. I cried rivers of tears.

"What's wrong Bella? What did I do?" Matteo became as sad as I.

"She's gone," I said.

"Who?"

"You can't know."

"Bella, you are healthy, you are getting stronger, be happy." Matteo turned his back on me for the first time.

"I can't," I said and looped some hair over the bald spot by my ear.

He grabbed me by both of my arms and stared into my eyes.

"You're a miracle case, the doctors said so. You are my miracle, Bella."

His eyebrow arched and he tried to snuggle me into the deep nest of his arms, but my body stiffened against him.

"What's it for?" I asked.

"We have a chance now," he replied, drawing away from me.

"I don't know." I left the porch.

The next day, I rocked in my old chair, feeling every bit of the rough wood against my spine, and scanned the street for Milady for the last time. I rubbed my forehead, traced my finger down the brim of my scar, and closed my eyes. Their insides were smooth and lit only by sunlight. I no longer could see the blood boil through the vessels or the atomic numbers that gave me comfort. And she was, simply, gone.

I walked back into the house and opened the closet. I took the gifts out and placed them on the table in front of Matteo. He looked up at me, an expression of hope in his eyes. I sat snugged next to him, and he spoke a single word.

"Bella."

He traced a circle on my thigh with two fingers and we ripped open the silver gift first.

Joel Lipman

Moo Cow

Once on the plume of dream white sleep, soaked with milk and shining through night, the moon came waving with lace. Her silver mantle bound all sides of that fair countenance. The lashes of an eye threw a shadow there. As white as snow in one night's fall, the moon of her sheen body shone outside her dress. White feet with rosy sandals rode a chariot of silver gold. Two braids of hair wound her head and one threw a shadow down her calves.

Frere Friedrich got it right. The Moon with her fresh Parthian lips should promise not to err the programmed path and its followers as well.

She is the cow of the world. You cannot name anything that is not a cow. The stars are cows that come at night and the moon is the great cow ooooooo. Just add an m. There Schopenhauer is weeping or we should say mooing. As Herr Nietzsche says, the world in suffering forgets and repeats the whole. It is triple speak to say, a cow is not a cow, but a girl, and the girl is earth. In this account of the Sue cow girl, Susan and the cow are speech and history itself with the allusion of everything glorious Wittgenstein said. But we cannot say and must not. In Susan space ships are cows and Fords. So you ask, am I a cow? Do you now remember friend? Do you remember it all? Herr Nietz in his last case said our cow was happy in its ignorance, but we empathize with Sue cow earth and the great oooooo more. Not to say the news is good, even if another Trump ensues, get out those prophecy books of the world cow now against its perps. Get'em up and read'em out. Now is the time to ooooooooooo you know.

The Remains on Danger Mountain

When the moon, the cow and Susan unslumbered from that night and headed west, moles had drilled the field and technologies the green. Hoboken east, west and beyond were all captive in this regard. Sue sailed the way ocean liners decline the horizon. It was a long going not yet given patrician cookery. She left behind the sea, volcanoes and glaciers of ice for microbursts, haboobs, tourists and temps. A mystical toponomy of opposites in the sleeves of her coat trod down alleys until she settled on the slopes of Danger Mountain. *Dangier,* in the French, from the Latin *dominus* 'lord,' in the original is a 'jurisdiction of a power to harm.' Sauntering upon her back came also the Belle Dam, our Madame Pop whose ziggurats and plateaus were the way Greeks made melodies in their art. Zarathustra came down that mountain too to the first town he would know. They thought he was a Clown, it says. Citizens then began chewing on their arms. Eating themselves before they were eaten by giants, for giants will eat ya, in case you're having a bad day. Rewire that brain to the Cow Becoming.

Here we sit together for a short prehistory in Egypt which Pied Cow carried in its bag. It carried the body itself, a chest with valuables of heart and lung like a decorated immigrant's chest. You are yourself that immigrant and carry yourself in a bag which inmost spiritual world has exhausted its outer forms.

A Cow of dark and light, to preserve a "society bred from youth grown up among us in the art of proving by words, multiplied for that purpose that white is black, and black is white" (*Gulliver*). A more literary Bruegel new worldliness set, fantastical forms to paint these Pied Cow states of its *new* world. Couched in dreamworlds every day, from the beginning grotesque to quackeries and libertines who say a ravenous

Uberman will appear, to write upon the skin of our cow a pied universe that cannot retain its past, Von Friedrich's peasant revels in dreamworlds. *Forward then enunciate, hail appoggiaturas, mordents and slur, let consonants range color, tone, pitch, break registry bid.* Fantastical forms and familiar bait to catch our uber, but not like a rat, beyond, *from the bottom, middle and top 'voice' call* to snatch the pillow-talk.

When your uber has arrived, the enemy ordinaire, set a familiar cosmic to create, in the uncanny hid, happy are we who wander the rumblings of this dark where Susan battled four-story myth. Would that fairy tales happened as they ought or old wives spin a thread to prove the best, but when her step mom slipped up to grind a gingerbread behind the absent King, Sue fulfilled the desire of patrician want. Please remember your terms in transfer of the theme. Susan is the world where Step Dame *spinnstubed* the world. Later Dame will offer a breath of TCE to intoxicate, but now Snow White, Riding Hood and Susan come in among mythogema and innocents. After a while she lifted up her head and ambled down the road.

The moon paused on the tops of Atlantic seascrapers that night, stationary on the western horizon line. When it did finally move, a cow remained, dropped off on top that building to the west. On its shoulders rode the man who is our due. He brought the Borealis current in his bag.

Electric in the barn, that cow in the field, under the tree, among the flocks stretched leaf with the heron that flies the canal. Pharaohs of the Nile rippled outward as she splashed. Other cows would shuffle through the hedge to put roses at her feet and take a seat to shade her eyes. Tracts of Red Hats then and night wind whispered to the wood gorse breath when she walked that rocky islet. Face to face men fell to their knees. Earth gatherers in the indicas of light confessed. They saw her white dress and breath of parted lips. Check a map for the best directions south. From Montauk down to White Bay streaks, where rooflines start and ferries and tugboats echo by night, Susan lived under Hoboken bridge.

Suzana Stojanović

Orange Tree

The tree barely stood because of the weight of the fruits. It seemed to me that it would break at any moment and that it would cover me. I waited for you for hours along with oranges the size of a soccer ball.

"You know I'm always late."

I know, but this was a dream. You could at least arrive on time in dream.

"I couldn't because your comprehension of me hasn't changed."

People came for hours and took away full bags. I wanted to keep the most beautiful oranges for you, but they grabbed them.

"You know I've never eaten fruits."

You should have. Maybe the cancer would encapsulate.

"It wouldn't. Everyone has a day when he has to leave."

Boris and his friends were sitting under the treetop. He didn't recognize me.

"Of course he's not because you've changed in thirty years, and he knows you the way he saw you before he left."

And I just wanted to talk with him.

"He wouldn't tell you anything new anyway except what you already know."

He never told me about his desires.

"I never told you about my desires either."

Yes, you are, about the house on the sea and about Montenegro, which we did not go to.

"We went with the thoughts, and that's something."

Those were our best days. Out of joy, we jumped into the war. At least we haven't lost our sense of humor.

"If we lost that too, what would be left of us?"

I can't even think about it. We would give up on dreams early. Everything would become a countdown.

"At least we didn't count anything."

Maybe we needed to — to extend.

"Everyone makes mistakes from time to time and has to start all over again. Something always rolls, like your oranges, so you lose track of the actual quantities.

Do you remember our story about the Earth and the Moon?

"That one day they will start to wear out and that darkness will eat them?"

Yes. We have always reduced science to a minimum in order to have as much time for nonsense as possible.

"Some things a man has to get out of life plan and program. Unfortunately, I realized that late."

I can throw out a lot, but not the trees. Somehow it all starts at its root, and ends at its fruit.

"That's why you dream about it all the time."

It seems — and always with ripe fruits. Behind this one, the orange, was your house, but different. You painted it orange and the windows green. A fat cat was walking on the roof.

"It, unlike women, was always waiting for me."

And really, you've never had any luck with women.

"And which musician did have? They gather like bees when they smell money, and disappear together with it. Anyway, tell me more about the dream. It's cold and boring here. Snow enters my bones."

I heard music. Boris was talking about a girl who drowned in a lake. They searched for her until morning. She didn't want to surface.

"There are deep lakes, in our valley."

Not as deep as unpredictable. Do you remember we called them martial?

"Yes. Many got into conflicts because of them. What else did you dream about?"

I snuck into the house.

"And when aren't you?"

I let the light in. I rummaged through the drawers a bit. In them I found my stories, the first, old ones.

"The first are the best, as is the first love, as paintings."

In the corner stood that thick orange guitar you sold to get rid of the memories. I looked around it a bit. I was trying to find out what was so special about it.

"It's nothing but a moment."

The moments passed very slowly while I was waiting for you. Krleža was on the shelves everywhere. I was wondering why you love him so much.

"It's because he connects the characters in a strange way."

You know, you took care of everything, but you left that old armchair in the middle of the house. The signatures of all those who sat on it fought on the backs. You also left a wall under the bar where we wrote poems so that our thoughts wouldn't take them away. You have preserved all our valuables.

"I preserved everything but health."

You haven't changed the big windows either. From them, you could still see the hills where cypresses hugged us. Accidental rain started to fall. Boris tripped over an orange and then I woke up. I picked up the phone to call you, but your number wasn't there.

James McNally

Brooklyn

He did not feel like he was dying but he wasn't quite sure and he likened what he was feeling to the sound of a series of doors slowly closing shut and echoing in a soon to be empty house and he struggled to see but there were bright lights in his eyes, fluorescent bulbs that painted everything in a washed out light but at the same time gave a harsh angularity with stark black borders to the surrounding objects and he could feel bustling movements around him and the sound of muted voices and when he tried to raise his arm he could see a wristband that said Fitzpatrick, Aiden A. but something or someone roughly pushed his arm down and he did not know where he was or whether he was awake or asleep and dreaming but the last he remembered he was living in Brooklyn and he could sense that some of these closing doors were still open and he remembered the promise he had made to himself long ago where he had wanted to write one story, one sentence or even just one word that would encompass his past and all that had occurred over the years and he felt he still had time so he sought to gather his thoughts as he did not know for certain what his future might hold lying under these lights and all these thoughts made him want to write about his times and he knew there were more stories locked up in his head and all he needed to do was to tease them out as the people were in there and the feelings were there as well, and it was left for him to remember and to put it all down somehow even though others had written about their lives and Brooklyn more eloquently than he ever could, but their experience was theirs and not his so he remembered what they had said was the best and most truthful way to do this was to just write and never take ones pen from the paper or hands from the keyboard never stopping for punctuation or grammar and just go with it to see what would come like snippets of memories or vignettes – little intertwining vines – snapshots that could become parts of larger stories from his times in Brooklyn to Elsewhere.

Stephen-Paul Martin

Song for Our Ancestors

I've just been thrown out of my house. The fight with my wife got so bad that I didn't even try to get back inside, either by sneaking in through a window or by shouting at the locked back door. So now I'm slumped in a chair on the back porch, warming myself with an old blanket, and I close my eyes, somehow drifting off to sleep in the chill of the city's thick fog. Then I'm wandering through the late night streets, looking at old houses and stores as if they were great works of art, fascinated by dormers, porticos, cupolas, gables, columns, transoms, bay windows and oriel windows, and other architectural structures I don't know the names of. I walk for hours with no destination, finally reaching parts of the city I've never seen before, streets with vacant lots filled with garbage, old brick warehouses with shattered and boarded up windows, silhouettes of factory smokestacks looming in the distance.

I reach the place where the streetlights come to an end, but the street keeps going. I keep walking. Soon I come to a free-standing door, apparently propped up by the fog alone, no evidence of a building having been there. It's made of light blue paneled wood, and I like it so much I can't keep myself from knocking. A voice invites me in, so I open the door into what looks like a recording studio. There are microphones, keyboard instruments, drum kits, guitars propped on stools and chairs, a mixing board against the far wall, beneath a clock that reads 3:15, and on a folding chair near the door a newspaper dated December 29, 1968.

I'm tired so I sit on the concrete floor, my back against the wall. I hear laughter and voices approaching, young men with long hair and thrift shop clothing. They don't seem to notice me. A guy with mirror shades starts playing with the mixing board, and slowly the room is filled with harbor sounds: seagulls, lapping waves, foghorns, ship's bells and buoy bells. A guy with a vest and an ascot settles in behind the keyboards, adding soft washes of symphonic sound that seem to go on for hours. I drift into sleep, wake briefly, see from the clock it's 4:45, hear the keyboard symphony swelling and surging, laced with gently distorted guitars and barely audible drumming. I fade back to sleep again, wake briefly, see that it's 5:35, hear the keyboard symphony surging and swelling, softly distorted guitars and subliminal drumming, glide back to sleep again, wake to a waterfront morning dense with fog.

I'm sitting up against a metal warehouse door. Everything is slightly blurred, but I let myself fully breathe in the moist air, and before too long I'm clear and refreshed. I get up and walk without knowing or caring where I'm going, but soon I'm home and Corina looks great, smiling at the breakfast table, telling me how worried she's been, asking me where I've been.

I say: That fight we were having last night was so stupid, I couldn't see any reason to come back inside and start arguing again.

She laughs: Sometimes you're the biggest asshole in the universe.

But I was trying to be nice.

If you have to try to be nice, something is wrong.

I always try to be nice.

It's not convincing. I can always tell what you're really feeling. You might as well just be honest.

Honest? Really? What if I don't like being honest? What if I think honesty is over-rated? What if I think I'm better off not being honest?

You've got a black belt in passive aggression.

At least I'm good at it. Anyway, I sure don't want to spend another night on the street. But actually it wasn't bad. It was like being in a dark museum.

A dark museum? How would I know what it's like to be in a dark museum?

Picture yourself in a museum with all the lights off. You know the paintings are there on the walls, but you can only make out vague frames and forms and muted colors, and there's no one else there.

Why would I do that? I like looking at paintings. Why would I bother looking if I couldn't see them clearly. They weren't made to be seen in the dark.

It's like being in a haunted house but there aren't any ghosts, so there's nothing to be afraid of, and you can just enjoy how weird the house looks in the dark.

Whatever. So where did you stay last night? An all-night fast food place? A Motel 6?

Nowhere. I just went. I didn't know where I was going. I just walked until I was back here again. It was like I was walking in my sleep, but I know I wasn't dreaming.

She gives me a funny look. But an hour later she's acting like everything's great. She's doesn't mind bad arguments because she's clever when she fights and doesn't hold on to shitty feelings once the conflict is over. I'm the type who feels disturbed after a fight and holds on to the feelings for hours, and sometimes for days, until I find some way way to distract myself, often by doing what I'm choosing to do now, sitting down at my computer and doing my freelance job, designing virtual environments for computer game companies. I'm working on one right now that includes a subterranean cave, walls filled with images that glow in the dark.

After dinner Corina wants to make love and as usual she's terrific in bed, strong and supple and skilled, so afterwards I'm convinced that our problems aren't as bad as they often seem to be. Then she's amusing me with her opinions about the President's latest absurd proclamation, how he thinks there's no such thing as global warming and how it's better not to regulate big corporations because then they get richer and give people jobs and the people have more money to spend, the ongoing capitalist bullshit that sounds especially misguided coming out of the President's big mouth.

But now she and I are falling asleep in each other's arms, something we've always done beautifully, probably the best thing about our marriage. Then it feels like something is easing me out of sleep and the clock says it's two hours later, 2:25. I see that she's sound asleep so I get up and go downstairs and think about making a snack. But then I'm focused on the street lights out the kitchen window, and something about the way they're receding into a mysterious distance makes me want to go out and start walking. I don't know where I'm going or why I'm going there. But something happened last night that I can't quite remember, a gap in time that I want to recover, assuming that gaps in time can be recovered. Or maybe they can only be reinvented, like dreams that change from poetry into prose when you try to talk about them later. Somehow it feels important not to know where I'm going, so I turn randomly down cross streets onto side streets, from side streets back to main streets back to cross streets back to side streets, all of them lined with brownstones and old brick buildings with gables and cupolas, until I reach the warehouse district, where the silhouettes of water towers and smokestacks tell me I'm where I was before. I recognize the stand-alone blue door in the foggy darkness. I open it quickly. I knocked the night before but this time I don't and this time there's nothing. Not even nothing. It's whatever makes nothing nothing. Not the word for nothing used in a sentence, but the nothing that makes the sentence itself impossible. I step back and turn. There's no safe way to keep looking.

I walk ten blocks to an old café, half-way below the sidewalk. I sit at a small circular table. There's a *Chronicle* on one of the chairs from December 29, 1968. There's a faded black and white picture of the Fillmore West on page 44, the Steve Miller Band on stage, performing what the reviewer calls a sound montage, a term I like, though I'm not sure what it means. I stare at the date. The paper was published more than half a century ago, the same day I took my first tab of acid. A friend had given it to me as a birthday present.

Footsteps approach and a woman sits at my table. She's got long red hair, torn black jeans, and a powder blue cowboy shirt. She pulls out a joint, lights it and takes a long hit, and hands it across the table. I take a brief hit and smile my thanks and hand the joint back.

She looks at me carefully, then says: You don't remember me, do you?

Actually, your voice sounds familiar.

Remember that trip we took to Timbuktu?

Sort of. I remember taking a trip there with someone named Elaine. I guess that's you? Sometimes I'm not even sure that really happened.

Trust me. It really happened. And my mother was your boss a few years before that. You must remember—

At the pet store? That really cool spaced-out woman was your mother?

Of course! What's happened to your memory? Too much acid?

That's one way of putting it.

You were quote unquote working at her pet store near the Fillmore, a year before it closed. She introduced us. I was getting my PhD in anthropology.

Oh yeah, that's right. And we went to Timbuktu because you wanted to study those manuscripts, and I had a strange meeting with a musician in a club on the edge of town.

You never told me much about it.

Things got weird. I think at some point I was lost in the desert.

I remember a call from a Red Cross mobile unit. I got you on a flight back home. You weren't the same after that. You got more serious. You stopped returning my calls. I remember you moved to New York to study computers. What are you doing now? Still into computers?

Kind of. I do virtual environments. Right now I'm doing one that has Stone Age cave painting imagery. But what are you doing here?

It's my favorite place. I get up at two every morning, since I do my best work in the middle of the night. For some reason, I can't get myself to work at home. But here, I can really get things done. I love the coffee. They've got their own special blend. You should try it! Anyway, when I saw you come in, I said to myself: Hey! I know that guy!

And then it all came back to me.

It's been decades, hasn't it?

It feels like another lifetime.

What are you working on?

I'm translating a pre-Islamic mathmatical treatise. I found it in someone's basement in Timbuktu. The guy who had it knew nothing about it. But he quickly examined it, made a face, and told me it was dangerous.

That's weird. How can math be dangerous?

I think it was a religious thing: pre-Islamic math instead of Islamic math. Math that the Prophet would have condemned, instead of what passes for math in mainstream schools.

Sacreligious math, not officially sanctioned? Math for dreamers? Is the treatise any good?

I've been working on it for decades. It's fucking amazing!

I've never been good in math.

Me neither. But the math in this treatise really gets inside your body. It's not just a mental thing. It's more like music. It takes you to places that don't even need to exist.

Sounds like my kind of math!

She hands me the joint and I take a long hit and lean back and close my eyes. When I open my eyes to pass the joint back, she's gone. I search the room. There's nothing but faint light coming from scented candles on the tables. The guy at the cash register is snoring into folded arms. I like how relaxed he looks, so I let him sleep. I step outside and look both ways but she's not there walking away. The only reason I know she was really here is the joint I'm holding. It's still smoking. I take a final toke, then snub it out on my jeans and put the roach in my back pocket. I feel so calm just standing here in the fog. Maybe if I never move again I'll be okay. But the emptiness of the streets, so enticingly defined by the streetlights receding into the darkness, tells me that I need to start walking, and soon I'm standing again in front of the blue free-standing door. This time I know what to do. I knock, like I did last night. A quiet voice tells me to come in.

I open the door into what looks like a recording studio: keyboard instruments, drum kits, guitars propped on stools and chairs, microphones everywhere, a mixing board against the far wall, beneath a clock that says it's 3:15, and on a folding chair near the door a newspaper dated December 29, 1968. I'm not sure what to make of the date. I was born on December 29th, and the paper is more than fifty years old. Why is it here? Why isn't it in a library or a museum? Why does the paper itself look fresh, like it's hot off the press? The headline mentions troops confronting rioters. I think of the Vietnam War. I might have been one of those rioters.

I'm tired so I sit on the floor. I hear laughter and voices approaching, young men with long hair and thrift shop clothing. They don't seem to notice me. A guy with mirror shades starts playing with the mixing board, and slowly the room is filled with harbor sounds: seagulls, lapping waves, foghorns and ship's bells and buoy bells. A guy with a vest and an ascot settles in behind the keyboards, softly replacing the foghorns with washes of symphonic sound that seem to go on for hours. I drift into sleep, wake briefly, see from the clock it's 4:45, hear the keyboard symphony swelling and surging, laced with calmly distorted guitars and barely audible drumming.

Someone sits down beside me and stares at the ceiling. I'm not sure what to say so I don't say anything. He finally says: This music is really awesome.

I say: I remember it from a long time ago, I think at the Fillmore West, but it sounds even more amazing now than it did back then. There's something psychedelic about it, but in a quiet way, not blowing your mind but gently taking it places, maybe to the border of silence, where conscious thought is still possible, but just barely.

He says: Psychedelic. I haven't heard that word in a while. But I can tell you about psychedelic, no question about it. I mean, I was wasting my life, becoming a total couch potato. The only thing I read was *TV Guide.* Then I answered an ad. At UC Berkeley they wanted volunteers, people to take psychedelic drugs and then get observed by bearded guys with flannel shirts and clipboards.

He takes an envelope out of his inner coat pocket, pulls out a page of perforated squares, and says: Ever try one of these?

I laugh and say: It looks like blotter acid. I haven't seen stuff like that in a long time.

The first time I sucked on one of the squares, I felt like I was back in the Stone Age, like I was in a subterranean cave, with strange equations painted on the walls.

Were they doing math back in the Stone Age?

I didn't say it was math. Just things that looked like numbers in patterns that looked like they might be equations. Not the stuff they used to make us do in school.

Equations without math?

Sure. Why not? It was back in the Stone Age. Who the hell knows what they were doing back then? Who knows what would have made sense to them, assuming that they cared about making sense?

He looks at me like I'm supposed to know what to say to that, but I'm barely awake and can't think of anything, so he nods and smiles and says: Everything starts right here, man, right here and right now.

It feels like I'm at the job I had a long time ago, surrounded by fish in beautifully designed fishtanks, parakeets and canaries chirping and singing, puppies and kittens playing and wandering freely, keeping everyone company, a store where people come and go without being pressured to pay for anything. They just sit and relax and talk pleasantly about things that seem to matter.

I close my eyes and the music is taking me back there, the bubbling of large aquariums in dim blue light. I slide into sleep again, wake briefly, see that it's 5:35, hear the keyboard symphony surging and swelling, softly distorted guitars and subliminal drumming, drop off to sleep again, wake to a waterfront morning dense with fog.

I remember waking up like this yesterday morning, after a night of wandering the streets in the warehouse district. Now I'm puzzled by the memory of a basement café, a *San Francisco Chronicle* from 1968, an article about the Fillmore West, which was closed on Independence Day in 1971, a place where I spent my seventeenth birthday, a memory enhanced by the blotter acid I'd been given by a friend. It's all blurring, like images in a dream before they get sorted out when you talk about them later. Was I in that basement café last night, and if so, why was I there? And why do I remember someone talking about equations in a subterranean cave? And what's my partner thinking now, since I've been out all night two nights in a row?

I get lucky. She's still asleep when I get home, and when I wake her up with my mouth between her thighs, she couldn't be more excited. She comes twice, then again when I penetrate her, thrusting fiercely to build a savage climax.

Resting beside each other as the dense fog presses on the windows, it's like we're in love again, though we both know the feeling won't last.

She laughs lightly: I like you so much more when you're fucking me.

I like me so much more when I'm fucking you.

I can tell. You're not such a passive aggressive creep.

I smile and stand beside the bed. If she knows I was gone the night before, she's showing no sign of it. We go downstairs for breakfast, open our laptop youtube account, and catch footage of a detention center on the Rio Grande, desperate faces pressed up against chain link fences. Then footage of the President bellowing about national security, drug dealers and prostitutes from degenerate nations flooding our country, stealing jobs.

I look at Corina: Drug dealers and prostitutes from degenerate nations? Does the man have any idea how stupid he sounds? Those people aren't in sinister gangs dealing drugs. They're trying to save themselves from gangs dealing drugs! And families are still being separated, two years after a federal judge declared the Zero Tolerance policy unconstitutional. What the fuck!

Corina says: He's such an offensive shit! And I'm never sure if he's just totally ignorant, or if he's playing dumb to manipulate public awareness. How long do we let this motherfucker survive?

We've waited too long already.

Where are today's great assassins when we need them? How long would Gavrilo Princip have tolerated someone like this.

Princip thought he had nothing to lose. He was dying of consumption, starving, living in borrowed rooms or on the streets.

But people like us have got too much to lose, right? We like our bourgeois comforts too much to do what needs to be done.

I take my laptop upstairs to the small room I use as an office. The fog is so thick at the windows it feels like it's in the room, making everything chilly and vague. I see the term "night terrors" on my newsfeed, and I click to the article, but get distracted by a distant memory, triggered by the woman I met last night in a basement café. I haven't thought about her in years, but now a strange trip we took is coming back to me in fragments. I'd first met her in the late sixties, at the pet store where I had a part-time job. She was getting her PhD at UC Berkeley. A strong attraction quickly developed, and soon we were thinking of moving in together. Then she told me she had travel plans that she didn't want to change, a trip to Timbuktu, a place that had once been one of the world's great centers of commerce and learning. I convinced her to take me along. I'd always thought the city had a cool name, but I knew from reading I'd done that the place was falling apart, fading into the desert, despite its fabled past. Elaine wasn't there for the fables. She was trying to get her anthropology dissertation started, and she wanted to see the hundreds of thousands of ancient manuscripts there, all kept in private homes in secret places, commentaries on every conceivable subject, so many things that people don't know anymore.

Things went well at first. The people were friendly, seemed eager to help, and we soon found a pre-Islamic text about sexual pleasure, positions and techniques we tried and enjoyed. But Elaine wasn't there for sex, and soon she was so caught up in her work that she didn't have time for anything else. We had several bad fights, which made it clear that we didn't have much in common. We said goodbye and I moved to a different hotel. I was left to explore Timbuktu by myself. But the place was way too hot, and aside from the ancient books, there wasn't much to explore. There were scorching winds, dunes closing in on all sides, streets that were buried in sand.

I spent most of my time in my air conditioned hotel room watching pornography. I ate cheeseburgers and French fries every day in the hotel café. I felt stupid. Here I was in a town that was once considered the African version of El Dorado, and all I wanted to do was play with myself. So a few nights before my departing flight, I walked through the older section of the city, patting myself on the back for not completely wasting the trip. But I quickly got lost on narrow unlit streets that all looked the same. The sand was so deep that the doors of the buildings were half way below street level. If I'd wanted to go inside I would have been forced down onto my knees to dig my way in.

I finally found normal access into a small cafe on the outskirts of town. The place was falling apart but they had live performers, two young women making music I found a bit strange at first, but the sound became intoxicating once I adjusted to it. Flute sounds were quietly mixed with subliminal drumming, gliding through the room like tropical fish in a huge aquarium, drifting out the open doors into thousands of miles of sand and wind and stars and nothing else. At times it felt like I wasn't wearing anything, or hearing anything for that matter, or like the music was coming from me, as if by listening to the sound I was creating it.

At some point there was a pause, though I wasn't aware at first that the music had stopped. It was moving through my veins. It was on my skin. It was in my breathing.

I sat on a bench in the corner watching shadows move on the walls. It felt like if I watched them long enough I would understand everything, all the arcane wisdom in the books of Timbuktu, though none of them contained a word of English. Then the drummer came to my table, took my hands with bedroom eyes, told me in graceful English to buy her a drink, then asked me about myself in a way that sounded like she cared. Our talking was playful and somehow familiar. We seemed to know exactly what to say to each other. Our legs were touching under the table. I sat eagerly through her second set, which made what she and her partner played before sound elementary, like a prelude to something developing into a prelude to something else.

Then we hurried down dark streets to her house, a place like nothing I'd ever seen before. It was all one room, lit by scented candles. The walls and floor were dried mud harder than rock, all faded blue. The windows were circular openings without glass. The ceiling was ten feet high made of branches and palm fronds woven together, stitched tightly enough to keep out the almost non-existent rain. She said the place had been in her family for countless generations, going back more than a thousand years, back to pre-Islamic times, when the town was nothing more than a seasonal settlement. She told me the music she and her partner played each night was sacred, something their ancestors needed to hear, an ongoing improvisation keeping the living in touch with the dead.

She knew from memory everything that was in the sexual text. I'd never gone to bed with anyone even half as good as she was, which surprised me because I'd assumed that Timbuktu was a religious place, too steeped in Islamic tradition to encourage erotic performance. But her big soft body moved with athletic power. I felt like I was wrestling with the ocean. I felt I'd been making love to her all my life and everything still felt new. We came together several times in different positions. The candles were making the walls come alive, as if their faded blue were like the sky, concealing a darkness filled with stars, constellations telling ancient stories.

At some point we passed out in each other's arms. I woke at four in the morning, ready for more of the best sex ever. But she wasn't there. The house wasn't there. The streets weren't there. Timbuktu wasn't there. I was in a small shed with a broken roof. The temperature had dropped at least fifty degrees and the wind was strong. The shed was falling apart and empty except for one crucial thing, a garment large and heavy enough to function as a blanket. It was smelly and torn but it kept me warm enough until the sun came up. Without it, I would have been frantically pacing, hugging myself to fight off the cold, right after spending four of the most ecstatic hours of my life. In the light of day, I saw that I was nowhere. I was lost and the desert was empty in all directions. At first I didn't care. Every cell in my body felt beautifully fucked. I snuggled back into the garment and let myself rest in the ripples of pleasure. I don't know how long I was there. At some point I was dreaming of a sinking ship, dolphins leaping and splashing in an ocean filled with ice. But finally something like hunger told me I couldn't stay there forever.

I wasn't sure what to do so I started walking. I turned around five minutes later, thinking I might need the garment again at night. But the shed wasn't there. I looked in all directions, blinking and rubbing my eyes. I knew the place wasn't a fantasy. The shelter and warmth had kept me alive. But even though I retraced my footprints carefully, back to where they began, there was no sign that a shelter had ever been there, no torn and smelly garment, only wind getting hotter by the second.

I walked for maybe an hour before I passed out. I woke in a room surrounded by concerned faces, nurses and doctors asking me questions, a Red Cross mobile unit. I wasn't making much sense, but I told them how to contact Elaine, and she figured out how to get me on a flight back home the next day. Back in the States, I was glad to be alive, knowing how close I'd come to being dead. I didn't understand what had happened, how much of it was real. But I didn't care. I was so relieved to be back in my normal life that I didn't even try to get in touch with

Elaine and discuss what happened.

Now I'm staring at my newsfeed, a scientific article explaining the term "night terrors," and I'm thinking about Elaine, the pre-Islamic math that she's been studying. Somehow the two things are connected, but I'm not sure how. Sometimes I wish I'd become a cognitive scientist, doing research on the architectures of consciousness, or maybe trying to identify the general activity, common throughout the universe, that human thinking is one specific example of. But I'm not sure thinking can be defined in architectural terms. Maybe it's more like a fishtank with boundaries that reshape themselves in response to what they're containing, an aquarium like a transparent water balloon.

For the next few days, my cave painting video project takes most of my attention. But Corina seems agitated, a bad sign. When she's in difficult moods, she takes them out on me. I try to fuck her into relaxation, but in bed she's ferocious, no tenderness at all, insisting on strap-on sex, taking me up the ass as roughly as possible. Then she flips out when she sees the President's face on our morning laptop, another molestation story, this one involving a teenage girl he supposedly called Lolita, though he seemed sincere when he claimed that he'd never heard of the book or its author.

Corina's spits on his meaty self-satisfied smile on the dusty screen. Speaking in her loudest, most powerful voice, she points at me and says: If you were caught fucking a teenage girl, you'd be behind bars in a second, no questions asked. But the president? If he even gets charged with anything, nothing will happen.

And he's claiming *she* seduced *him*. Can you believe it?

You men are disgusting. It creeps me out to think I'm not a dyke any longer. I'm sleeping with the enemy.

I'm the enemy?

You know what I mean. Oh, I meant to ask you: Who's Elaine?

Elaine?

Yeah, the one who texted you.

Texted me? What are you talking about?

She picks up my phone from the kitchen table and pulls up a text and reads it out loud: Great being with you last nite! Good to see you're aging so well! CU soon! –Elaine.

I don't remember giving her my number, but she got it somehow and now I'm fucked. There's no way to make what really happened seem plausible. I quickly say: When you threw me out I didn't know what to do, so I just started walking, stopped in a café, and ran into someone I used to know.

At three in the morning? Really? You're so full of shit. You're just as bad as the asshole in the White House.

That's hitting below the belt.

So to speak.

I can see that she's just about to blow up. Her fists are clenched and her face is red. I don't want to get slapped. I'm afraid I might hit back. So I grab my coat and go out the back door without saying a word.

I take a room in a small hotel three blocks away. It's a nice little place but the bed feels wrong and I toss and turn for hours. I keep thinking about the night terrors article, a term the author kept using: "the alternative past," memories based on things that really happened, but available to us now only in reconstructed form, as partial events overshadowed by vivid images, which initially were just background details, though now they've taken center stage and we can't get them out of our minds. I can't remember the author's discussion clearly. It's like I'm getting more and also less than she intended, like I'm telling someone about a dream but I know I'm getting it wrong, making it sound more coherent than it really was. Finally I fall asleep but then I'm awake, moving quickly out through the lobby into the street, rushing past the desk clerk sleeping on the job, face down on a newspaper crossword puzzle.

I'm feeling unhinged, but the fog calms me down, and soon I'm caught in the rhythm my footsteps make. If I had to state a religious preference, I'd say I believe in walking. There's almost nothing better, especially when you don't know where you're going and don't want to. The old brick buildings make the fog seem fluidly sculptured. The fog makes the buildings drift, makes them seem closer and farther away. Time is nothing more than the sound of my shoes against the pavement.

When I see the blue panel door, I think at first that it must be part of a building. But then I see that there's nothing but the door, floating in fog. I know I've been here before, but the only thing that comes to mind is the back door of the Fillmore West, July 5, 1971, the night my friends and I tried to break in after the place was closed for good. We couldn't believe it would soon be a used car dealership. We were stoned and wanted to spend the night on the stage where our favorite groups had played. I remembered the Steve Miller Band, their sound montage that lasted all night, the amazing transformations in the way the guitars and keyboards sounded, something more than music, or maybe I was just on some really great acid. When I think about the lame big hits that later made Steve Miller and Boz Scaggs rich and famous, I want to put my fist through the door. But instead I just knock. I think I hear a voice telling me to come in.

I open the door into what looks like a recording studio. There are keyboard instruments, drum kits, guitars propped on stools and chairs, microphones everywhere, a mixing board against the far wall, beneath a clock that says 3:15, and on a folding chair near the door a newspaper dated December 29, 1968. I'm tired so I sit on the floor. I hear laughter and voices approaching, young men with long hair and thrift shop clothing. They don't seem to notice me. A guy with mirror shades starts playing with the mixing board, and slowly the room is filled with harbor sounds, lapping waves and seagulls, ship's bells and buoy bells and foghorns. A guy with a vest and an ascot settles in behind the keyboards, softly adding washes of symphonic sound that seem to go on for hours.

I feel myself drifting off. Then someone's beside me, long red hair and a cowboy shirt and sandals. She's in the lotus position, which doesn't seem right for the way she's dressed. The music swells and slides from side to side like I'm on the deck of a ship, or like I'm in a cave surrounded by images in torchlight. She pulls out a joint, takes a long hit, and slides it into my hand. I take a brief hit and smile my thanks and hand the joint back.

She says: Nice to see you again.

How did you get my number?

I just tried the one you had thirty years ago, when we took that horrible trip. It's weird that you've still got the number you had before. How did you manage that?

It wasn't easy. But what are *you* doing here?

What are you doing here?

How did you know where to find me. I wasn't planning to come here. I'm not even sure where we are. My wife saw your text and got mad. I had to get out.

I'm not surprised. The last time we saw each other back in Timbuktu, we had a bad fight. Do you always fight with the women you're with?

I shake my head, laughing: It's really weird. In principle, I refuse to approach any situation that's likely to produce a disagreement, especially an intense disagreement, and I resent it when people try to create tense situations. Yet I seem to choose such people as romantic partners.

Why?

I'm an idiot.

It sounds like you should write a book about how to avoid relationships. There are so many books about how to find the right person. You should write about how it's better to live on your own.

I'm sure someone's already written a book like that. In fact, if I did a quick Internet search, I'd probably find at least five books on the subject. Besides, I don't have enough experience to write such a book. I always end up in relationships, even though I know they suck. Like right now, I'm liking the way you look, and I'm thinking I might want to get you in bed, even though I know how bad things were before, when you threw me out of our Timbuktu hotel room. It's like I don't learn from experience. How can you write a book when you haven't learned anything?

She pats my back and says: I don't go to bed with men anyway, not anymore. So don't worry about it. Just listen to the music.

Her face slowly blurs into something I think I recognize, a face that takes the form of all the faces I've forgotten. I drift into sleep, wake briefly, see from the clock it's 4:45, hear the keyboard symphony swelling and surging, laced with gently distorted guitars and barely audible drumming, then glide off to sleep again, wake briefly, see that it's 5:35, hear the keyboard symphony surging and swelling, softly distorted guitars and subliminal drumming, fall off to sleep again, wake to a waterfront morning dense with fog.

When I get home, Corina's sleeping on the couch with the TV on. The TV's never on, except to watch movies, which we only do once a month, if that. Sometimes I think we should just get rid of it, since we can watch movies on our laptops. Corina used to watch Cable News because she had a crush on Beth Barton, the glamorous picture tube journalist, or at least that's what Corina repeatedly told me, trying to make me jealous, and when I agreed with her that Beth Barton was hot, Corina got nasty, claiming I was imagining Beth Barton during sex. That was the end of TV news for both of us, and I don't miss it at all, especially not the commercials. But now the set is back on, though at least the sound is off.

I take a closer look. Instead of morning news, the tube looks like it's become an aquarium. It's filled with the graceful motions of tropical fish. The only sound is the bubbling of the filter, which reminds me of the pet store I worked in back in my late teens, a small shop near the Fillmore West. It wasn't just a place that sold animals. In fact, few animals were ever sold. It was more of a place to hang out surrounded by dogs and cats and birds and large aquariums of tropical fish. I remember sitting on the floor with friends and complete strangers having stoned conversations about *The Politics of Experience, One Dimensional Man, The Joyous Cosmology,* and *The Doors of Perception,* books we only vaguely understood but enjoyed talking about at great length, discussions filled with laughter and confusion, playful arguments that didn't go anywhere and didn't need to, people pausing half-way through their sentences to watch the fish in their tanks, thirty minutes later picking up right where they left off. No one was entirely sure who the owner was, but a woman who liked wearing cowboy shirts was there all the time and seemed to be in charge, though she was never bossy. We were all half in love with her, but everyone somehow knew that it would have been wrong to say it out loud. It was just that she had such a range of relaxing facial expressions, such cheerful and generous body language, that no matter who you were, you would want her to care for you for the rest of your life. She never said much about herself, but she was fond of mentioning that her ex-husband had supported himself in college by volunteering for tests in which he dropped acid and then got observed by men with clipboards. She didn't seem to be managing much of anything, but she always played the most relaxing music, something that began with harbor sounds, slowly replaced by symphonic keyboard atmospheres of various kinds, mellow jazz guitars and soft drumming, the same music I heard that night at the Fillmore, that sound montage by the Steve Miller Band, years before they sold out. It's weird to think that she was Elaine's mother and the blotter guy was Elaine's father. She might have been born with "Song for Our Ancestors" playing softly in the background, ambient music before the term become popular.

Now I'm watching the fish while Corina sleeps, not sure why the pet store memory seems so important, like a dream I can't quite get myself to interpret, knowing how different the interpretation would be than the dream itself. Something happened last night, and the night before that and the night before that, something about a door in the fog, a group of young men playing music. I'm glad that the picture tube is filled with fish. I'm glad there won't be any more news or commercials. The world has been sold and sold and sold and sold, and now it's not worth much. But music remains, and it's nice to think that we don't need anything else.

Robert James Cross

Emergence

Fundamentally this is an art-historical document about dreamers having the ability to transcend space and time with "lucidity," and the apparent danger this presents to the government.

—The text begins with forged CIA documents released to the public describing a study on lucid dreaming. The unforged study was to determine whether a dreamer can communicate with other dreamers in the facility or with those outside the laboratory setting.

— Next is a chart of different dream states and their connection with psychic phenomena.

— Next is a journal entry from the 18th century where the writer describes communicating with one of the dreamers from the contemporary study, and having it ripped away by the CIA scientists waking the dreamer as the person from the 18th century looks on.

—Next is the transcript of a human who worked on the project phoning a paranormal radio show and trying to get information out about what occurred during this study and others before it.

—Next is a court transcript in a case against the CIA about what occurred during the study.

—Next is every drawing from C.G. Jung in his *The Red Book: Liber Novus* layered on top of one another to create a stamp.

—Finally, is the termination wherein the CIA agency and its scientists claim absolutely nothing occurred.

TECHNICAL PROTOCOL: ANAMOLOUS COGNITION IN REM STATE

DRAFT

I. OBJECTIVE

The objective of this investigation is to determine if anamolous cognition can be observed during lucidity in the R.E.M. sleep cycle.

TECHNICAL PROTOCOL: ANOMALOUS COGNITION IN REM STATE

DRAFT

II. BACKGROUND

Dreams involving anomalous cognition (AC) have been a part of every human culture from the times of Ancient Egypt to the present. The first serious attempt to examine AC in an REM state under controlled conditions began under the direction of Montgomery Ultman, MD in 1963 at the Community Mental Health Center of the Mount Sinai Hospital in New York. The research of AC in dreams continued until 1981 where the REM procedures were abandoned in favor of a simpler and more rapid approach to the study of AC. Heinrich Karl Chinaski has summarized and critiqued this body of research in the American Psychologist.

In the studies, individuals were asked to sleep in a laboratory and be monitored for brain activity and eye movement. From these records, it was possible to tell when they were in an REM state. Upon the onset of Rapid Eye Movement (REM), a laboratory technician would notify a viewer, who was isolated in a containment facility, to begin focusing on a randomly selected target. At the end of the REM period, the individual was awakened and asked to report the content or visions they experienced during their REM state. This procedure was repeated throughout the night using the same target material for each separate visionary period (e.g., up to twenty). The final assessment of the AC content was accomplished through an independent panel. As described by Chinaski, significant evidence for the validity of AC was observed under a variety of experiments.

The individuals in these studies were not always focused upon the AC task. They slept as usual and reported their dream content. In our pilot study, we will focus the dreamer explicitly on the AC task using the methods of lucidity. A lucid dream is one during which the sleeper becomes consciously aware that the experience is a dream as opposed to the subject being awake. Dunberg et al. (1985) found that it is possible for individuals to know when they are dreaming and to signal subjects in the waking world, through predetermined eye movements, indicating cognitive awareness during sleep. Using this ability, Dunberg et al. (1987 and 1990) conducted a number of psychophysiological studies to determine the differences between waking and dreaming from the perspective of the individual.

They found that sleep is similar to the waking state. Motor action is mostly inhibited from the brain stem downward; however, the cerebral cortex appears not to "know" this or "accept" it as such.

In this preliminary pilot study, we will use the skills developed by Dunberg to teach individuals to lucid dream. Differing from the earlier AC dream studies, our subjects will be instructed to adopt a proactive attitude to seek out and remember the AC target. In this way, we will determine the degree to which lucid dreaming can facilitate the reception of AC material and how an individual in REM sleep can interact with it.

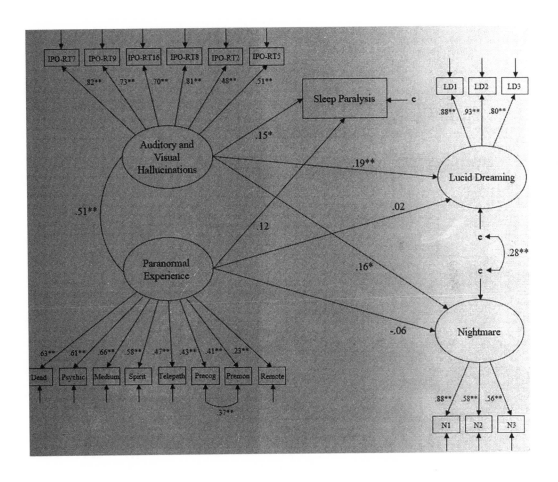

June 18 1863

Still I think of her. My vision blurred in the summer haze when I hear her name on the tongues of the men who killed her. I pray for one more lifetime by your side.

My love. My heart. My soul.

I dream of the white room from which we met — in memory it remains.

The men with their coats dragged you into the darkness. Your screams haunt my every moment.

Close mine eyes so I may see thee

Close my heart to all others

I pray we sleep — The future is dark

Jeff: On my CIA line, you're on the air, hello.

Male caller: Hello, Jeff?

Jeff: Yes

Caller [sounds frightened]: I don't have a whole lot of time.

Jeff: Well, look, let's begin by finding out if you're using this line properly or not.

Caller: OK, the CIA?

Jeff: Yes. Are you an employee or are you now?

Caller: I'm a former employee of the CIA. I, I was let go on a medical discharge about a week ago and, and... [chokes] I kind of been running across the country. Damn, I don't know where to start, they're, they're gonna, they'll triangulate on this position really soon.

Jeff: So you can't spend a lot of time on the phone, so give us something quick.

Caller [voice breaking up with apparent suppressed crying]: OK, um, um, OK, what we're thinking of as aliens, Jeff, they're extra-dimensional beings, that, an earlier precursor of the CIA they made contact with. They are not what they claim to be. They've infiltrated a lot of aspects of, of, of the military establishment, particularly the CIA.

The disasters that are coming, they, the military, [long pause] I'm sorry, the government knows about them. They found out about them through dimensional dream communications with the beings. And there's a lot of safe areas in this world that they could begin moving the population to now, Jeff.

Jeff: So they're not doing, not doing anything.

Caller: They are not. They want those major population centers wiped out so that the few that are left will be more easily controllable...."

[Broadcast begins to break up]

Jeff [fragment]: ...discharged...

Caller [uncontrolled sobbing, then fragment]: I say we g.....

[Dead air]

THE COURT: AND YOU WERE MADE AWARE
OF THESE ██████?

DEFENDANT ████: THEY WERE GIVEN
AMPLE COMPENSATION IN THE AMOUNT
OF $██ FOR THEIR MONTHS IN THE
██████.

THE COURT: THAT WASN'T THE
QUESTION MR. ████. THE QUESTION
WAS WHETHER OR NOT THE ██ KNEW
ABOUT THE ██████.

DEFENDANT ████: WHICH? THE ██
CENTURY ONES OR THE ONES FROM THE
████?

THE COURT: EITHER.

DEFENDANT ████: WE KNEW ABOUT THE
████ ENTITIES BECAUSE OF OUR OWN
████ CONDUCTED WITHOUT THE USE
OF GUIDED MEDITATION. THE ████
USED DIFFERENT CHEMICALS TO INDUCE
LUCIDITY IN TEST [CONT]

22

IV. DISCUSSIONS AND CONCLUSIONS

The purpose of this investigation was to determine if AC was possible in a lucid dream state. Because the trials were conducted in supervised and sterile conditions, it is possible that the target material was compromised by our presence. By using standard meditation techniques, compared to previous attempts using galantamine, lucid dreams are less frequent and of a shorter duration. All subjects reported restful and uneventful sleep during the study. Thus we were unable to prove AC in a state of lucidity as no subject communicated with one another or the control subjects located on the opposite end of the compound.

Knowing the historical effects that AC had on many different cultures we are unable to conclude whether or not these tales from textbook and lore are subjective circumstantial evidence. If the lucid dreaming effect sizes were larger than historical and emperical evidence using galantamine, the study would have broadened to a greater number of agency laboratories.

Robert L. Penick

Dream State

He thought about how, if he had a wife, he would be very quiet slipping out of bed at two in the morning. Padding down the hallway, he would flip on the kitchen light and pour himself a glass of milk. So quiet he could hear his own breath. Extinguishing the light and taking a seat in the living room. Through the big bay window, the driveway and front lawn would rest warm in the porch light. It would reek of permanence, the grass blades remaining their exact length for an eternity. Nothing moving, like living in an untouched snow globe.

Sitting still, in that chair, he would sip at the milk and recount various episodes of his life, the memories coming in no particular order. Perhaps the first game of little league, when he struck out twice, but managed an infield hit before the rain moved in. Or Ms. Dedmon, the petite high school English teacher, her calves straining as she conjugated verbs high up on the board. Christmas. Springtime. His mind would pass over events like fingertips on a keyboard. When the milk was gone, he would rinse the glass and leave it in the drainer, then tour the darkened rooms, touching the edges of artwork and the corners of tables.

When his fatigued returned to him, he would check the front and back doors to make sure they were locked, rinse his mouth in the bathroom, then glide back toward the bedroom. For a couple of minutes he'd stand at the foot of the bed, watching his wife sigh through her mouth. Then, sliding beneath the sheet, he would fall back into the rhythm of time.

Robert Boucheron

The Writer in the Tower

Carl Gustav Jung was born in 1875. As a boy he lived in Hüningen, a suburb of Basel, on the Rhine. In his 1961 book *Memories, Dreams, Reflections*, he says, "My way to school led along the river." As he walked, Jung constructed a fantasy of a castle with a moat, a wooden bridge to a gate flanked by towers, and "a tall keep, a watchtower. This was my house."

The interiors were plain, the defenses were strong, the library was excellent, and the tower had a secret: a copper column or cable from the roof to the vaulted cellar, to gather from the air "a certain inconceivable something" and conduct it down to a laboratory. The fantasy had weapons, cannon, soldiers, council sessions, and a sailing ship, and Jung was the "arbiter" of all. After several months, though:

> I found the fantasy silly and ridiculous. Instead of daydreaming I began building castles and artfully fortified emplacements out of small stones, using mud as mortar—the fortress of Hüningen, which at that time was still intact, serving as a model. I studied all the available fortification plans of Vauban and was soon familiar with all the technicalities. From Vauban I turned to modern methods of fortification, and tried with my limited means to build models of all the different types.

Sébastien de Vauban was the chief military engineer to Louis XIV, and Basel lies just south of Alsace, which the king annexed to France.

As Jung describes his solitary play, the reader thinks of sand castles, snow forts, model train layouts, and construction toys such as Lego bricks. They excite the imagination and make long hours fly. Play at building can be solitary or social, as in a kindergarten class or at the beach. The fascination is individual and nonverbal. It is about solid geometry and using objects to represent ideas—in a word, sculpture.

In his account of building model fortifications, Jung exaggerates. Did he really master "all the technicalities" of Vauban's plans? About ninety pages farther on, he records another memory which sounds like this one. He says that at age eleven:

> I had had a spell of playing passionately with building blocks. I distinctly recalled how I had built little houses and castles, using bottles to form the sides of gates and vaults. Somewhat later I had used ordinary stones, with mud for mortar. These structures had fascinated me for a long time. To my astonishment, this memory was accompanied by a good deal of emotion.

"Somewhat later" may refer to the castle-building at age fourteen. The writer in old age may be confused, or he may have played at building throughout childhood, inside the house and outside, using whatever materials came to hand. As a grown man of thirty-seven, Jung wanted to recapture the boy's state of mind.

> I began assembling suitable stones, gathering them partly from the lake shore and partly from the water. And I started building: cottages, a castle, a whole village. The church was still missing, so I made a square building with a hexagonal drum on top of it, and a dome. . . . I went on with my building game after the noon meal every day whenever the weather permitted.

Jung lived his adult life mainly in Zurich. From 1900, he worked as a doctor in the Burghölzli Mental Hospital. He married well in 1903, and when his father-in-law died in 1905, Jung became part owner of the International Watch Company in Schaffhausen, a thriving business that ensured the family's financial security for decades. Jung neglects to mention this economic detail. He says that he resigned as senior physician at Burghölzli in 1909 because his private practice as a psychiatrist had grown so busy. He was also a lecturer and then a professor in psychiatry at the University of Zurich from 1905 to 1913.

In 1923 at age forty-eight, Jung began to build a house at Bollingen, on the north shore of Lake Zurich. To this house he devotes a chapter called "The Tower." Jung begins by noting his "scientific work" of recording "fantasies and the contents of the unconscious." Then he says:

> Words and paper, however, did not seem real enough to me; something more was needed. I had to achieve a kind of representation in stone of my innermost thoughts and of the knowledge I had acquired. Or, to put it another way, I had to make a confession of faith in stone.

Construction continued at four-year intervals. Jung's description of the Bollingen Tower is vague, more symbolic and emotional than physical: "the feeling of repose and renewal that I had in this tower was intense." Photographs show a small, picturesque castle built of rough stone painted white, with pointed roofs of slate or tile, and a courtyard. It stands beside the water on flat ground, not on a hill or a peninsula, and trees rise above the landward side. There is no moat. The original round tower is squat. It has two stories and tiny windows. Jung says:

> At first I did not plan a proper house, but merely a primitive one-story dwelling. It was to be a round structure with a hearth in the center and bunks along the walls. . . . But I altered the plan even during the first stages of building, for I felt it was too primitive.

Instead of a fortification, the Bollingen Tower is a parody of a castle. Jung took it seriously, and he identified with his house. After his wife died in 1955, "I suddenly realized that the small central section which crouched so low, so hidden, was myself! So, in that same year, I added an upper story to this section." The addition is in half-timber and stucco with a large window. At the age of eighty, "it signified an extension of consciousness achieved in old age."

The house had room for others. It was a family vacation spot, after all. In the end, it became a family shrine. Shortly after Jung built his final addition: "I chiseled the names of my paternal ancestors on three stone tablets and placed them in the courtyard of the Tower. I painted the ceiling with motifs from my own and my wife's arms, and from those of my sons-in-law." The old man grieves for his wife and reflects on those who died long ago. But the medieval bits and the bourgeois striving for social status are a throwback to the late nineteenth century, when Jung was young.

In *Memories, Dreams, Reflections*, Jung does not connect the house to his bouts of model building in childhood and again at age thirty-seven. Yet it strikes the observer as more of the same. The writer builds a house in an archaic style with stones beside the water. The Bollingen Tower is privately owned today, not open to the public.

* * *

Hermann Hesse wrote the essay "On Moving to a New House" in 1931. It is a brief history of the houses he lived in up to then, where they were, what he was working on at the time, with whom he lived, and so forth. The style is playful. Hesse wants to convey the impression of a hedonistic, carefree life. Yet he certainly had problems.

Hesse was born in 1877 and grew up in Swabia in southern Germany. He rebelled, ran away from school, dropped out at sixteen, floundered, and attempted suicide, as he says in "Life Story Briefly Told" of 1925. For eight years starting in 1895, he worked for booksellers in Tübingen and Basel, long hours and grinding labor. His first wife Maria Bernoulli suffered from poor mental health, which strained the marriage and him.

From 1904 to 1912, Hesse, his wife, and their three children lived in the German village of Gaienhofen, on the north shore of Lake Constance. They rented a farmhouse for a few years. Then in 1908, using money from his wife's parents, they built a new house designed "by an architect friend from Basel." Hesse describes each in detail, along with the beautiful rural setting. Of the farmhouse he says:

Something that no later house could give me made this farmhouse precious and unique in my eyes: it was the first! It was the first refuge of my young marriage, the first legitimate workshop of my profession, here for the first time I had a feeling of permanence . . . Here for the first time I indulged in the beautiful dream of creating and achieving in a place of my own choosing some kind of home, and it took shape with meager and primitive means. . . . The arranging of this house was done with the fine pathos of youth, with the feeling of our own personal responsibility for our actions and in the belief that it would be for our whole lives.

After an initial literary success with the novel *Peter Camenzind* in 1904, Hesse's high moral and political stands alienated many in the German-reading public. From 1914, as an outspoken critic of militarism and war, he was a pariah. *If the War Goes On: Reflections on War and Politics* is a collection of his short essays from 1914 to 1948. Addressed primarily to Germans, the essays speak to all Europeans and Americans today. By way of vindication, Hesse won the Nobel Prize in Literature in 1946.

Hermann Hesse and Carl Gustav Jung were contemporaries, born and raised in the same geographical area. Swabia borders Switzerland, and Hesse lived with his parents in Basel, Jung's hometown, from age four to ten. The two writers met in 1917, as Hesse got psychiatric help from Josef B. Lang and Jung. The writers became friends. Some critics detect a Jungian influence in Hesse's novel *Demian*, written in 1917, and in later work.

Formed in the same cultural mold, Jung and Hesse shared an interest in dreams, the psyche, development of the individual, European folk culture, Eastern religions, and the fringe realm of parapsychology—magic, séances, foretelling the future, uncanny coincidences, and fate. In particular, both writers drew from their intuition and emotions. Hesse's novels and stories are autobiographical, as he realized in 1921: "And all these stories were about myself, they reflected my chosen path, my secret dreams and wishes, my own bitter anguish!"

Hesse lived in Bern during World War I, in the "haunted house" of friends who had abruptly died. He worked as a volunteer for the German Prisoner-of-War Welfare Organization, managed two newspapers for prisoners, and edited books for them. In 1919 he found the peace of mind he sought in the Italian Swiss town of Montagnola, where he rented rooms in an old house called Casa Camuzzi. Here he stayed on and off for twelve years. This was a productive period for his painting and his writing, which included the novels *Siddhartha* in 1922, *Steppenwolf* in 1927, and *Narcissus und Goldmund* in 1930. This brings him to the year he is writing the essay. In 1931, when he turned fifty-four, he married Ninon Dolbin, and they moved to a house built for Hesse by his friend Hans C. Bodmer.

In a fond farewell, he describes Casa Camuzzi as "the imitation of a Baroque hunting lodge" and "this half-stately, half-droll palazzo."

> The door of the house opens pompously and theatrically on a princely stairway leading down to the garden, which with many terraces, stairways, scarps, and ramparts continues until it loses itself in a ravine . . . From the valley below as it peers out over the quiet wooded ridge, it looks with its spiral staircases and little towers exactly like a country castle out of one of Eichendorff's novels.

Photographs show that Hesse scarcely exaggerates. The crow-stepped gables, pink stucco, and tangle of vines give Casa Camuzzi a whimsical air. It appears as a setting in his fiction, and he drew and painted it several times. He notes fallen trees in the garden and remodeling over the twelve years:

> But none of these alterations changed my affection for the house, it was more my own than any of the earlier ones, for here I was not a married man and father of a family, I was alone and at home.

Casa Camuzzi is privately owned today. In a tower of the building, the Hermann

Hesse Museum opened in 1997. A photograph taken inside shows a desk facing a Gothic arched window thrown open to the garden, with a little balcony. A typewriter sits on the desk, and photographs of the author hang on the walls.

* * *

The European writer is partial to towers. Michel de Montaigne in the 1500s created a library in a tower of his chateau, as he tells us in his Essays. Sir Walter Scott completed Abbotsford in 1824 as a "medieval" country house with turrets and battlements. Alphonse Daudet published *Letters from My Windmill* in 1869, the return address being a stone tower in Provence. For six nights in September 1904, James Joyce stayed in a round stone tower in Sandycove, near Dublin. He then used the setting in the opening of his novel *Ulysses*. Buck Mulligan and Stephen Dedalus wash and dress one morning, look over the parapet, and eat breakfast "in the gloomy domed livingroom of the tower." Vita Sackville-West lived in the Tudor tower of Sissinghurst Castle from 1930 to 1962, and she replanted the garden.

William Butler Yeats's summer home from 1917 to 1929 was a medieval tower in County Galway, Ireland. Yeats published a poem called "The Tower" in 1928. Carl Jung shared Yeats's interest in spiritualism and medieval lore, but he began his Bollingen Tower five years before. Hermann Hesse mentions the "little towers" of Casa Camuzzi in an offhand way. He dwells in a tower but does not dwell on the fact.

Like a prehistoric standing stone, the tower suggests a person. Embedded in a city wall or a church, the medieval tower often has a name. It may have a gate at the bottom like a mouth, and a peaked roof on top like a head. The tower is tall and proud, an image of defiance, safety, and solidity.

In the mystic realm, the tower and its occupant merge. The tower suggests the isolation of the writer at work, alone at a desk, shut away from the world, in a room like a cell. Finally, after the writer dies, the tower remains, a monument, a work of art.

Nick Sweeney

Magic Pictures – a Dream of the Eastern Roman Empire

(Chapter 84 of the unpublished novel Istanbul Song)

"So you're the storyteller of Byzantium now, Aidan, are you?" Ayşenaz closed her eyes. Turkish moons appeared either side of her mouth and by her eastern nose; she was beautiful, caught in the strange light from the continent across the water. "You're a strolling player now, telling tales? I love your tales," she said softly. "I always think I know them, but they twist and turn and always surprise me."

"Nobody knows them." I trapped her hand, saw its lines trailing off on stories of their own. I plucked her fingers like the strings of an instrument and she seemed to like that. "They're locked in my head. Nobody knows them until I tell them, but... Shall I tell you a secret?"

"Tell me."

"Well then, walk with me awhile and I'll tell you. Will you do that?"

"I have work to do." She pulled impatiently at her sleeve. "And I'm in my work clothes."

"That's not important."

"Well, where shall we walk?"

I don't know where we walked. The streets were packed with the scum of the eastern empire, noisy and violent with commerce, busy with diseased camp-followers and drunken soldiers and smug priests about their business, all bushy beards, bulbous noses and red-rimmed eyes that stared at us for seconds as we passed.

Ayşenaz said, "Where?"

"There." I pointed. I promised her I knew our road. Byzantium was a sprawling jumble of bricks set with muck, impossible structures that ultimately defined streets smelling of peelings and animal insides and urine. There was the grand road that led from the triumphal arch set in the walls to the great church, there were the fine forums marked by their free-standing columns fallen to ruin – it was no longer a time of columns – there were the streets full of artisans' workshops, and of shops, the paths that led off to imperial palaces fast disappearing into the tenements. We went through the oldest quarters, stayed in backstreets made of mud, full of timber houses that would burn down or harbour foul diseases until they were ready to eat us away. "That's why we have to live now," we agreed, knew that there would be no other chance, not till we got to Heaven. Nobody knew how long that would be. I told Ayşenaz about how Saint Paul said this and Saint Paul said that about Heaven, the *evidence of things not seen,* but I didn't know about that, not really. He was history, Saint Paul, was he not? Who remembered him? "Only you." Ayşenaz laughed at the idea, looked like a child then and declared, "I love to laugh."

We were in fearsome places where nobody laughed. I felt nervous, but shied away from sshing her out of my own lily-livered caution.

The world was different when I walked with her. It didn't spin so quickly and violently; everything looked different, felt different, was recalled in a different way. I loved her, I knew in my heart when we walked together not touching, when I was able to look around and see her next to me. I don't know where we walked. Perhaps it wasn't there at all, perhaps it was somewhere else. Perhaps it wasn't us at all, for I let all sorts of people wander through my head in the night as I lay dreaming, or as I sat up and smoked and drank chocolate milk, imagining.

I picked up pictures of her. There she was on the Galata Bridge looking moody as she thought about forever, in the background the Yeni Cami and the air moving with pigeons. There she was, moody in Yesilköy, the air empty of planes. And there on the ferry to Asia Minor, her front bright with flowers in which still breathed the sweet air of the Aegean and the petrol fumes of the road. There she stood in Byzantium, in the Tekfur Sarayı, a palace built for doomed emperors, lips pursed for a kiss. Then on the walls built by Theodosius when he was just a boy, a wisp of hair escaping from her French plait. There, in the big bank on İstiklal in her bank clothes, helping customers' faces fall. And in Amasra, shaking loose from her sweater, her hair going this way and that. I spread the pictures with a flourish like Tarot cards, in my hands and across surfaces. I scattered them in the air, let them fly around my head, tore them up, used magic stolen from the Field of the Genie to piece them together and change them, magic pictures; I had magic pictures of Ayşenaz that turned to *cinema verité* behind my eyes where she'd once lived.

It wasn't true that I didn't have a camera. I did, a bulky Russian SLR that I hated the look and feel of, a sign you hung around your neck saying *I am a train spotter.* It followed me around the world like a beggar I'd insulted once. It had sat in drawers in Paris and Berlin, and lay now in a stinky duffle bag, its single eye shut as I saw Asia Minor and walked in the Garden of Eden, crossed the Hellespont by boat, came back again and again to ancient cities, Chalcedon, Galata, Scutari, Byzantium.

The pictures I took were in my head with the other junk. Who'd want to look at them? You want a picture of the Aya Sofya? Well some geek with enough equipment to fill a swimming pool has been there first, made a picture, had somebody put it on a postcard for you. But he didn't take any pictures of Ayşenaz. If I'd had a picture of her I'd have sat up nights staring at it, a graven image. That wasn't healthy, was it? It was ridiculous. I was glad I didn't have to do it, I supposed, but was never quite convinced.

Wasn't I an iconoclast anyway, tearing up pictures of my lost love Marie-Hélène the night we got back in one piece from Kütahya? Yes, that was me: iconoclastic, beetle-browed, Byzantine, burlesque.

No, Ayşenaz would live on in my head for a while, come to life there and hold my hand and pucker her lips to kiss me, she'd pull her sweater off, again and again, would undo the zip on her skirt, let it fall, would make her cunt open like a flower. Then she'd stop doing those things, move out of my head, sit in my heart, a small trace of her.

For now though she's beside me near Saint Saviour in Chora. We stop in its garden and listen to the solemn bells of Byzantium, look out on the domes of churches built in the name of the God we cherish under different names and fear in our bones. Even if He is good.

"What was the secret?" She tugged hard on my arm, made me stop and look at her.

She'd walked with me a long way, past the open cistern of Aspar and the crumbling church of the Holy Apostles, and we were out by the city walls watching a wailing family bury a child who'd been kicked to death by a horse. We wandered on, saw workmen raising a new palace for the thirteenth apostle and his family, those born to the purple – "*Porphyrogenitus*," I told her, but she didn't know any Latin at all, and thought I was speaking baby-talk.

"There's no secret," I had to admit. "I just know what I know here in my head and I tell what I tell and… that's all there is." I took her hand again and she resisted, pulled instead on my arm, reached out and swung me round on the spot and smiled and ceased to care about there being no secret to take back. I remembered then that she wouldn't be staying, had to go through the sea walls and back across the water. "No secret." My smile went. "I'm sorry. I just wanted you to walk with me through this city of ours and remember me this night when you sail over to Scutari, to remember me every night, should something terrible happen in these dark times in which we live, and you never come back to Byzantium again."

otHer

faCes

disappEar

Joel Lipman

Benjamin Abtan

The Third Child

"I had to move to save my other children," Hnina whispers. "Yaacov, your father, did not want to leave his beloved red city. He said that we had to stay strong for your two brothers, that other children would come, with the help of God. But deep inside, I knew I had to change something. I knew we had to change cities to protect the children we had, and those who might follow."

Leah listens silently to her mother. The small room is dark, lit only by the smooth flame of a half-burned wide white pillar candle placed on the wooden table at which they are sitting. The shutters have been closed to prevent the strong light of the Casablanca afternoon sun from entering. Pause. In the silence, Hnina and Leah can hear only from a distance the lively agitation of the narrow white mellah streets packed with traveling traders, men in European suits on their way to business meetings, and children in light dresses, shorts, and leather sandals coming back from school with their family's Arab helpers. Leah looks at her mother's tears invading and disfiguring her face, like a sudden and silent tsunami. This is the only moment of the year when she sees her sad - Hnina is usually so joyful, smiling, carefully listening to the other mothers at the open-air market where they go together! Today is the day for mourning Leah's brother. Their annual secret memorial day, and the first time she has heard such a story from her mother.

Leah never knew this brother - she was born after he passed away - but she often thinks of him. Sometimes, at night, when her brothers Doudou and Jojo have fallen asleep in the bedroom they share, Leah speaks with him: "Where are you now?", she asks. "What would we do, if you were here with us, with me?" Sometimes, she hears his responses, in a distant and childish voice, and they have a conversation until she falls asleep without noticing it. Sometimes, he does not answer. "He must be playing with his friends there," she thinks.

She discovered his existence, and his disappearance, three years ago, when she was eight. On that April day, she arrived home after being picked up from school by the old Mahmed, in his ample white wool djellaba, his head covered by its qod, the baggy hood, to protect him against the burning sun. Like every day, just after entering the house, she took off her sandals to prevent dust from entering. In her white short dress and barefoot, she was about to run to the kitchen and grab the fresh pastries that Hnina and Fatima, her helper, prepared every day for the children, when her mother suddenly appeared at the front door. She was wearing a traditional dark blue velvet kaftan embroidered with gold, when she usually wore simple long cotton dresses with light colors. Hnina summoned her, very briefly: "Come!"

Leah was frustrated. She loved these pastries so much, especially the dates and the figs stuffed with marzipan! But her mother's tone and attire were unusual. She seemed nervous and in a hurry, when she usually appeared so much in control of her time, of her house, and of herself. Hnina took her energetically by the hand into the parents' bedroom. Leah was surprised: this room was a forbidden place in the house, like a sacred sanctuary. She had been told on several occasions, when she had wanted to sleep in her parents' bed to be protected from the djinns that invaded her nightmares, that once children were no longer babies, they had to sleep in their own room, that this place was for parents only.

Why, then, were they sitting in her parents' bedroom now? For some reason, Leah felt she had to keep silent when Hnina, agitated, standing, apparently searched for something among her clothes in the closet.

"Here they are!" Hnina took a wide white pillar candle and a few matches out of her heavy winter fur coat. "We are going to light a candle and think of your brother, poor boy, may he be happy where he is," she added, as if to herself.

"What is she talking about? Doudou and Jojo are on their way from school, and they're not poor, they're like us," Leah thought. "Why light a candle for one of them? And for which one? Why?" The mystery, the hurry, and her mother's unusual behavior surprised Leah, and even made her a little fearful. She instinctively felt that she had to listen, without asking any questions, to avoid bringing more chaos to this moment and to her mother's heart. The atmosphere of this candle lighting was very different from the other kind she knew.

She loved it when, for as long as she could remember, her mother took her in her arms to light the shabbat white taper candles on Friday evening. That was a moment for them, for the girls. She was proud to do it with her mother, like an adult, in the kitchen flooded with light, next to the living room and its large table covered with the scented traditional meal composed of several salads of baba ganush, shakshuka, slow-cooked eggplants, beetroots, and grilled peppers, with spicy fish and beef in red sauce waiting on the hot plate on the side to be served, in an orderly manner, the one after the other.

This candle lighting in the bedroom was different. It was as if she and her mother were hiding. Just the two of them, in the dark. They did not loudly say *Baroukh ata…"* so that everybody in the house could hear the blessing and understand that shabbat had entered and that it was time to come together for dinner. Instead, Hnina slightly bent over the low wooden table, quickly mumbling words that Leah could not hear, as if they were thieves. "Please light the candle, Leah," Hnina suddenly asked. Leah had never seen her mother like this. She was impressed by the strangeness of the moment. She mechanically lit the matches and the candle. "That's fine. Let's go now," Hnina said

right away, already standing, taking Leah's ha
don't tell anybody. This is only for us, girls."

"But Dad is going to see the candle when he
careful to respect the unspoken rule to not
willing to support her mother.

"He is away for two days, he will come back after
out," Hnina responded. Leah was used to this, her father
two or three days to sell jewels in the towns surrounding Ca
remote cities. He always returned before shabbat on Friday night, w
for Doudou, Jojo, and herself. "Please go, I'll be there in a second," Hnina said,
quickly closing the parents' room door.

A minute later, Hnina joyfully welcomed her eldest son, David, and his younger
brother, Joseph, at the front door, with a smile, now wearing a long cotton light
green dress: "Welcome boys! How was your day? Don't rush to the kitchen, take
your shoes off first! And leave some pastries for your sister!"

Leah had already rushed to the kitchen to make sure she could choose the best
pastries. After her first bite into the stuffed fig she managed to grasp, the marzipan
slowly melting and spreading its sweet taste in her mouth, she thought: "Who
is this brother? Why must I not tell anybody?" She was tempted to share these
questions with her brothers, to whom she was used to telling her stories of the
day, when her eyes crossed the deep gaze of Fatima, who stood in the corner of the
kitchen. In those dark, still eyes, Leah saw an unspoken "You have to keep it for
yourself!" She felt an invisible membrane separated her from her brothers.

first sudden ceremony with Leah, Hnina decided to tell the story
She's eleven now, she's mature enough to understand," she said to
ugh the religion sets the majority at thirteen for boys and at twelve for
lt this was the moment.

every year, she waited for Yaacov to be away for a few days. The Pessah holiday
ason was good for business, with its large family reunions at which new purchases
could be seen by all, although nobody showed them, out of humility. During his trips,
Hnina could say prayers for the soul of her beloved third child, Isaac, and light a candle
that could burn entirely before her husband came back. For this year's ceremony, she
had thought carefully of what she would tell Leah.

When Isaac passed away, after just twenty-two days of life, she remembered what her
own mother had told her, once, in a whisper, when she had given birth to Joseph, her
second child. "Pay attention to the next child, Hnina. Isaiah, my younger brother, the
third child of the family, died when he was eight years old. Suddenly. Like in a flash. I
loved him dearly, and I miss him every day of my life. In our family, the third children
are at risk. My mother told me so, once. We cannot change it, but our duty as women
is to do anything to take care of the children, particularly the fragile third ones."

When she gave birth to Leah, a year and a half after Isaac's passing, it was clear to her:
"She has to know. She is the only girl in the new generation. She has to protect the
lives of the children."

Every year, Isaac's passing anniversary makes Hnina relive the painful memories of this
terrible day again, as if it were today: "I am sorry, Hnina, this is meningitis, he had
no chance of survival," Doctor Assor had told her on that day, sitting in the bedroom

where Isaac had slept with her and Yaacov since he was born. "My condolences, Hnina, Yaacov. May God provide you with many more children!"

Hnina could not believe it. He was so lively, just two days ago! So lovely, too! She knew him already, she could feel his tenderness, and the fragility of his character. She felt him. Yaacov and she cried a lot, discreetly, alone in the room, sitting on the bed, wrapped in each other's arms, over the tiny baby basket and the still body of their newborn. David, then four, and Joseph, nearly three, could not hear any sound coming from their parents' bedroom that afternoon.

After two hours, the rabbi arrived. As was usual in Marrakesh in these cases, the Doctor had warned him of a death in the community. "R'bi Moshe", as he was called, was dressed traditionally, with a large green djellaba, like most of the Jews who lived in the mellah.

Mahmed and Fatima opened the door, and Yaacov came to greet R'bi Moshe before they entered together the room where the body had been lying for two hours. Hnina was sitting on the bed, like a statue, in the dark green wool skirt and long-sleeved cream-colored blouse she had been wearing since the morning. Silently crying, she had not been able to stop watching the tiny body of her child.

"Slama Hnina, I'm sorry," R'bi Moshe said. "Slama," Hnina responded, with a low voice, in a breath. Yaacov offered him a chair. He sat in front of Hnina and Yaacov, less than a meter away, with the baby basket between them.

"This is very painful, I am terribly sorry… I was so happy for his brit mila, just two weeks ago… God has given, God has taken back, we all need to accept this, even when it is the most painful thing in the world," he continued. "We need to begin the preparation for burial," he added. Yaacov and Hnina were not surprised by the hurry: they knew Judaism commands the burial of a dead person as soon as possible, on the same day if that can be arranged. They held their silence out of respect, and of sadness. R'bi Moshe paused.

"Yaacov reminded me the baby was twenty-two days old," he continued. "In that case, the Law is clear: there is no mourning. The parents and siblings don't have to stop listening to music or eating meat. In fact, it is an obligation for them to not stop doing so."

"Why is that?" Hnina asked, in shock.

"This is the Law, Hnina. According to the Wise men, before the age of thirty days, it is as if the child does not have a soul. So not mourning is an obligation," R'bi Moshe explained.

"My dear baby, no soul? How dare you? How dare you, men, what do you know about it?" Hnina wanted to shout with rage. But she was exhausted, and she knew she could not win this battle. She said nothing and could not hear anything else afterwards. Her eyes, usually so full of light, were wide open, still, wet, when R'bi Moshe, accompanied by Yaacov, stood and left.

Two hours later, Isaacs's tiny body was covered by the ocher earth of southern Morocco.

* * *

Now that Leah is eleven years old, Hnina has decided to tell her the story. "One night, a few weeks after God decided to bring your brother Isaac close to him in heaven, I had a dream. That confirmed my intuition that we had to change something. A wise rabbi appeared and gave me an order: 'Hnina, you have to move. You must leave Marrakesh to save your other children'," Hnina tells Leah. "I told your father the dream and the wise rabbi's order. I told him that we had to leave, to change cities, in order to avoid the curse that is upon the family and protect the lives of the children."

This is the first time Leah hears this story. Since their first secret memorial ceremony, three years ago, she has asked her mother questions about this older brother she never met, when nobody, or only Fatima, was in the house with them. She has felt a different connection with her mother than that of her brothers: she can ask questions, freely, like an adult. "And Dad, what did he say then?" she asks.

"In the beginning, he was reluctant," Hnina responds. She wants Leah to know the story and to pass on the secret to the succeeding generations of girls, so she has been glad of her curiosity over the past years, and of these shared moments. "All his business was in fabric, for which Marrakesh is the capital, and it's never easy to start a new business from scratch. Changing cities was a risky move, which could put the family in a difficult financial situation. But I was convinced that this was the right move to make, and I kept repeating my dream to him. I kept repeating that the rabbi was absolutely certain of himself, and that we had to obey him. 'We have to leave Marrakesh,' I repeated to him. 'God will provide us with what we need.'"

Her mother telling her about this conversation with her father makes Leah feel a little ill-at-ease, as if she has inadvertently entered the intimacy of her parents. It reminds her of that afternoon last year, when she was walking in the corridor to knock at the door of her parents' room and ask for their permission to play outside with her friends. Less than two meters away, she saw the door ajar, and heard a burst of loud voices coming from within. Discreetly, she came close and had a quick look inside: both Yaacov and

Hnina were standing, close to each other, speaking with large gestures. Immediately, she shifted her position and leaned on the white wall, her feet on the floor stones on which Doudou, Jojo and she were used to spraying water before sitting on them to cool down during the stifling summer afternoons. She could not be seen, but could hear everything Yaacov and Hnina were saying.

"No, I have not told anybody," Hnina said, apparently infuriated. "Your honor is safe," she added with a bitter irony.

"This is not about my honor, this is about respecting the rules," Yaacov replied curtly. "Do you think I am happy of it?"

"I don't know, Yaacov, you never tell! For years, you have refused to speak about it with me!" Hnina was obviously exasperated, nearly shouting.

"But I think of it every day!" Yaacov screamed. Leah was afraid, it was the first time she heard her father scream. She sweated, her heart pounding in her ears.

"He was my son too, Hnina! I loved him deeply, like the others! I think of him every day, and it feels like someone is peeling my skin." Yaacov's voice was much lower. The light crunch of their old wooden bed. Someone had sat down on it.

"But what can I do?" he said in sobs. "I have to go on, every day, to work, to make the business successful, to provide you and the children with all that you need for a happy life."

Another light crunch of their bed. The other person had also sat down. Silence. Low noises of fabric rubbing. Sobs.

"I love you," Hnina said. Leah had to listen carefully to hear her, because she said it in a very low voice.

Silence.

"It's OK if you do it Hnina. I understand you. I deeply feel you. I just don't want to do it myself, that would destroy me. And that's against the rules decided by the Wise men. I couldn't do it and still feel comfortable serving as one of the leaders of the community here," Yaacov added. "But do it, please. Do it for both of us. But when I'm not here."

Leah was overwhelmed. She had never suspected that her father could have such deep feelings. She had never really thought about it, in fact. She felt sad, and guilty. She wanted to enter the room and hold them in her arms, but that would have revealed that she had spied on them. With a heavy heart, she walked back silently to her room.

This year, Hnina goes on telling the story to her eleven-year-old daughter. "A few months after I had the dream, we moved to Casablanca, to this very house where we are now and where you were born, a little more than one year after." Hnina wants to make sure Leah has learned well the main lessons: "Do you understand, h'bibi? When it's necessary, you need to change. Changing cities may be hard, but in our case, the move provided protection to your lives. God willing, they will be protected until you are one hundred and twenty years old." This was a powerful statement, Leah knows that one hundred and twenty years is the maximum a human being can live, it is written in the Torah.

"To protect the lives of children, you must be ready to do anything. Especially for the third ones, like your brother, may his soul be in peace. They are particularly fragile," Hnina adds. She hopes Leah deeply understands despite the fact that she does not tell her everything.

What Hnina does not tell Leah, or not yet, is how insane she became when she lost Isaac. How strongly she hated men for imposing such inhumane rules like forbidding to grieve a lost baby. How deeply she was enraged by their lack of understanding and respect for what it is to be a woman, and a mother. The tensions with Yaacov, every day. The nightmares, every night. How she suffered to pretend that everything was fine and smile, outside, out of dignity, when she was falling apart, inside.

Hnina does not tell Leah that their Marrakesh house reminded her of Isaac in every moment, that this was unbearable for her, and that Yaacov could not understand it.

She does not tell Leah, and she may never tell her, that in fact she invented the whole story of the dream with the rabbi. "These men obey only rabbis and 'Wise men'," she had told herself. "They will never listen to me. I have to make up a story, this is the only way for me to be able to move and save my other children from the sadness and craziness of this cursed house." Hnina does not tell Leah that she decided to violate the Law decided by the Wise men, out of love, to commemorate her beloved son, every year, like all the souls who leave this earth. She does not know that Leah suspects this already, since she overheard the intense conversation with Yaacov last year.

Hnina does not tell Leah how she has been suffering, like in a constant and endless exile, for being so far away from Isaac's burial place, nor does she tell her of the secret nightly last visit she paid to him, on the eve of their departure to Casablanca, with the help of Fatima to climb over the cemetery's walls.

Hnina does not tell Leah all of this, but she has high hopes that her daughter understands the message, and that, in her turn, Leah will do anything to protect the children, especially the fragile third ones.

Listening to her mother, to what she says and to what she does not say, Leah strangely feels a light weight on her shoulders. Is it the sense of responsibility toward the children of the next generation, or is it fear for herself, now that she is the third child of the family?

Sara Jacobson

Cotton Candy Hills

If the definition of sleep is consciousness practically suspended, and suspended is defined as hanging, then hang I do. I hang on to the back of your waist, clutching you, yelling over the roar of the motorcycle engine. "You're going too fast!" I hear distant laughter as we course over cotton candy hills under bright blue skies. Lucidity proclaims *don't get on the bike, Sara.* You know better. West Side Highway. Three cars ahead. Motorcyclist hit. Man catapulted ten feet into the hazy summer air. Mass shock. We need an ambulance. Laight Street. Lucidity cannot stop me from riding on your motorcycle. I climb on, like chasing a moving train, the dust kicking up in its wake. My stomach drops as we hit the first hill and I question as to why I boarded in the first place. Do now. Think later. Curiosity. Impulse.

My Fitbit informs me that I am in REM sleep for 11% of the night. Although it cannot reveal the exact moment in which I slide into a residential street on a warm, summer afternoon. This time, I am watching you walk away. Maybe I should rephrase that, this time. We both know it's not just this time. Just as you reach the corner of the cobblestone sidewalk, a woman reaches out to you.

She's the wife of a friend of mine. Lucidity tells me I'm dreaming about her because Facebook invaded my psyche again. The birth of her baby girl plastered all over the news feed. You turn around and we lock eyes. I point to my eyes, then to yours. *Don't do anything bad.* You walk away.

At least you're alive in that dream. Because last time, I had to deliver the Heimlich

Dream maneuver and I couldn't save you. You fell limp into my arms. I had a terrible day. My Fitbit informs me that I am a light sleeper. Says I travel from light to REM. It also says not to worry, that light sleep is good. My Fitbit is trying to make me feel better about living a double life. There is the one in which you text me. You're sad. You're angry. I give you all the space you want, but you'd rather take up residence in mine. Then, the other state. The state that is housed between my ears. The state of self-torture.

I told you about the time I couldn't save you. We were in your Subaru, or was it mine? You opened my glove box and found a massive stash of super plus tampons and my face turned pink. I felt required to explain that the compact ones do not work as well, but that they were amazing at cleaning up spilled drinks in the console. You just couldn't believe how absorbent they are. I assume whenever you think of my car now, you think of feminine products. Which wouldn't be all that terrible if the razor and tweezer weren't also in there. You tell me that your ex kept condiments and utensils in your glovebox, the one prior, a hairbrush. I wonder if you think that this will make me feel better. You make a throaty uh huh when I relay the dream and I know you're judging me or psychoanalyzing me. My words are vomit.

I tell myself that I can drive you out of my dreams. I tell myself that I can drive you out of my dreams — drive you out of my periphery. Maybe there are three states. Dream. Reality. Daydream. If the dream states sandwich reality, yet take up more space than reality, in what sense do we exist in reality?

Sometimes it's like we are two pods on the same stalk, I text you. Same bean. Same pod. you respond.

I wonder what kind of suicidal bean this is. Cut one. Cut both.

It's a sentiment that feels disingenuous to describe. It's like speaking about something metaphysical over Pina Coladas. But I watched you walk over to the casket. I watched as you got on bended knee and mumbled something prayer-like. The magnet in me pulled towards your direction. _Stop it. Stop it._ You walked over to me thereafter. We left together. You had been shutting me out for weeks. It was cold outside. New York Winter. When we reached the parking lot you asked, _where are you headed now?_ Your absence made me angry, and in the anger, I misinterpreted as to what you were inquiring. _I am heading to my car._ I walked away from you. I walked away from you when I didn't wish to.

The daydream would have squared up differently. You would have pulled me back. You'd have said say something like, _I'm sorry I fucked this up. I want you._ In my dreams, you never say anything of the sort.

I roll over and open my eyes. _You were smiling in your sleep,_ my husband says. This time there was a party in the ocean. When low tide approached, it revealed a concrete pool, filled with saltwater. Like the sky on the morning of impending snow, you can feel it, but there's nothing to touch yet. You were somewhere in the periphery, but nowhere to be discovered.

That's odd that I was smiling, I answer. _It wasn't a good dream._

Robert James Cross

Mark DiFruscio

Land of the Heart's Desire

Renault: And what in heaven's name brought you to Casablanca?
Rick: My health. I came to Casablanca for the waters.
Renault: The waters? What waters? We're in the desert.
Rick: I was misinformed.

–Casablanca (1942)

I came to New Mexico for the aliens. Arriving in Taos, I discover that today is the last day of the Lilac Festival. Late to the party I have missed the pet pageant, a live performance by the Zephania Stringfield Band, the Tío Vivo Carousel (for kids), a flower planting booth, and the annual Taco Cook Off. All that remains are the vendors lining Civic Plaza Drive for the Arts & Crafts Fair: a street-long aisle of foldout tables under white canopies.

I swim down-stream with the other souvenir hounds, inspecting ceramic pots and handcrafted jewelry. I take a closer look at a cerulean blue metallic bracelet that the vendor fits it to my wrist before I can flee or protest. A moment later I've got my wallet open and he's instructing me not to remove the bracelet for two weeks if I want its healing powers to work. He then hands me a pamphlet explaining how "Magnetic Therapy" can reduce pain and generate healing—*Scientists have established beyond any doubt that all living cells are electrical in nature.* I'm not sure that all the pamphlet's claims have been scientifically verified. It warns, *Without pulsed energy there is not life.*

That night I sit outside on the back porch of my hotel room under a cloudless starfield, the emptiness beautiful and lonely. Before going to bed, I decide to heed the pamphlet's instructions by not removing the bracelet for two weeks, just to be safe.

*

Rick: If it's December in Casablanca, what time is it in New York?
Sam: My watch stopped.

*

I had other reasons for coming to New Mexico but mostly it was the aliens. I saw *Close Encounters of the Third Kind* for the first time as a kid and the idea of stepping onto a waiting spaceship to escape the lonely tedium of daily life held such an appeal for me that it bordered on religious ecstasy. A summer writing retreat in New Mexico seemed like a good place to learn more about alien experience phenomena, and maybe even catch a glimpse of a UFO. According to a 2015 Yahoo article, the public generally thinks of New Mexico as, "where meth is made and where everyone has been abducted by aliens." UFO sightings in New Mexico date back to the 1880s, part of a prolonged wave of "airship" sightings during the turn of the century. By the 1950s, UFO reports became ubiquitous in New Mexico, coinciding with the state's role in the birth of the atomic bomb at Los Alamos, and the development of nuclear and military installations at White Sands, Dulce and Albuquerque. One-third of the state is owned by the federal government, which makes New Mexico especially fertile ground for conspiracy theories: Roswell, cattle mutilations, underground bases, the "Taos hum" (Google it). Not to mention a disproportionately high number of UFO sightings—New Mexico's population of 2 million people ranks 36th in the U.S., but the state is 8th in UFO reports.

At the same time, the self-proclaimed Land of Enchantment has long been a magnet for artists, outcasts and visionaries. Henry Shukman writes in his *Guardian* piece "New Age New Mexico" that New Mexico is the "natural home of the fad… Bracelets imbued with Pluto energy. Crystals to make your carrots grow. Deep-core body-work. Whatever new 'spiritual technology' might be making tentative inroads into West Coast life 1,000 miles away becomes mainstream here." Part of this may stem from New Mexico's longstanding reputation as a place of healing, which, like its UFO sightings, goes back to the 1880s. The tuberculosis epidemic of the latter nineteenth century prompted doctors to recommend that sufferers relocate to dry, sunnier climates, like New Mexico. Called "the heroic cure," it was thought that TB "lungers" needed fresh air, exercise and sunshine.

I'm not a lunger, but a few weeks before coming to New Mexico I experienced my first full-blown anxiety attack and I'm still coming to terms with the cause. So maybe I also came to New Mexico for a dose of "the heroic cure." Failing that, there's the meth and aliens.

*

Renault: Did you have a good night's rest?

Laszlo: I slept -- Very well.

Renault: That's strange. No one is supposed to sleep well in Casablanca.

*

My second day in Taos begins with a flurry of graupel (like hail but apparently different because they call it graupel) which aborts my efforts to explore the local bookshops with a friend from the writing retreat—a Disney Adult who also struggles with anxiety. As the summer graupel intensifies, my Disney Adult friend and I huddle together on the front porch of a bookshop run by SOMOS— Society of the Muse of the Southwest—a nonprofit that supports the literary arts in Taos. SOMOS opened a bookshop in the town's historic district, the property having been purchased through donations from "fellow book-lovers, poets, storytellers, novelists– in short – SOMOS friends!" Unfortunately, SOMOS (like just about everyone else in Taos) call it a day at 4pm, leaving me and Disney Adult locked outside the front door watching Civic Plaza Drive get pelted by tiny ice pellets.

Sheltering from the weather, we peruse the FREE BOOKS on display outside. My Disney Adult friend picks up a Donald Duck picture book titled <u>Across the Big Country</u>, An Alphabet Adventure. "Across the Big Country," she says. "That's me. Travelling across the big country. This is the farthest from home I've ever been. Unless you include Florida. Obviously, I've been to Disney World."

"Obviously," I acknowledge, recalling that she worked for the theme park.

Still perusing books, I come across one that interests me called *Friendship: How to Have a Friend* by Adelaide Bry.

"Where's the farthest you've travelled?" Disney Adult asks me.

"Peru."

"Peru. What brought you there?"

"My partner is Peruvian," I say. "Also, the aliens."

With a laugh she asks, "Do they have aliens in Peru?"

"That's what they say. But I guess it's like what they say about God. If they're anywhere they're everywhere."

I skim contents of *Friendship* and discover a list of friendship possibilities I never knew existed: "Chapter I: Do You Take Friendship for Granted? Loneliness—The Other Side of Friendship. Chapter II: How to Get a Friend and Be One. Where to Find Friends/Courtship of Potential Friends. Chapter III: Your True and 'Not-So-True' Friends. Chapter IV: Man-to-Man, Woman-to-Woman, Black and White, Lovers and Ex-Lovers," etc.

Once the graupel clears I go back to my hotel and receive a text from my God &

Football friend in Texas. These are two of her major passions in life—college football on Saturday, and church on Sunday. I'm pleased to read that the hydrangea I gave her as a birthday gift has unexpectedly returned to life; she thought she watered it to death during the winter. God & Football friend seems to invest this development with a deeper spiritual meaning that alludes me. She goes on to describe a troubling dream that she had about me after the last time we saw each other. "You had been sick, but your dog got out and you went looking for it," she recounts via text message. "Then I saw online that you'd been killed by a car." She says how heartbroken she was over my death, but nobody seemed to understand or sympathize with her feelings. She tried talking to her priest, but he was too busy with other parishioners to counsel her. Her major concern was for what would happen to me because I don't believe in God. "I wanted to know if we'd end up in the same place. But then I heard your voice telling me not to freak out. And that you still cared about me, even though you were gone… Then I woke up and cried for like 20 minutes."

I wonder if this is my friend's way of saying that she is worried about me due to my recent anxiety attack. I reply with a single heart emoji, which seems inadequate to express how what she has written has touched me, but also seems appropriate in its wordlessness.

In *Friendship* Adelaide Bry observes, "The best elixir is a friend." Her definition of a *True- Blue friend* being someone with whom you *are on the same wavelength*. You might disagree about politics, religion or other beliefs, but you share a similar attitude toward life, and follow "the electricity of each other's thoughts," supplying whatever you find fun or stimulating or meaningful.

The always quotable Ursula K. Le Guin says it differently: "Two amoebas having sex, or two people talking, form a community of two." In "Telling is Listening" Le Guin writes, "amoeba A and amoeba B exchange genetic 'information,' that is, they literally give each other inner bits of their bodies, via a channel or bridge which is made out of outer bits of their bodies... sending bits of themselves back and forth, mutually responding each to the other. This is very similar to how people unite themselves and give each other parts of themselves—inner parts, mental not bodily parts—when they talk and listen."

I wonder what parts of myself I have given to others—hopefully some good bits. Fidgeting with my cerulean blue magnetic therapy bracelet, I skip the stargazing. Any interested aliens can wrest me from bed.

*

Renault: As I suspected, you're a rank sentimentalist.

*

Day four in Taos and still no aliens. According to the National UFO Reporting Center State Report Index for New Mexico, the most recent sighting was April 15 at 8:30pm in the town of Fairacres. The sighting lasted 30 seconds and involved three pulsating fireballs that glowed orange, red and yellow before disappearing into the Organ Mountains.

"I had just flown in from San Diego," the witness describes, "I stepped outside to look at the stars...for 33 years I have always looked up at the New Mexico sky knowing that someday I would see a UFO. And finally, there it was... I could not believe what I saw or felt...the only other experience that would capture the feeling... that feeling you have inside where you have 'a knowing' that this is something bigger than you."

So far, my only UFO sighting has been the little stickers affixed to Cattle Crossing signs along the highway. The stickers are placed above the cattle insignia to make it look as if a cow is getting beamed up into a flying saucer. I look into it and find recent visitors to New Mexico posting about the stickers on tripadvisor.com: "Curious about all the cattle crossing signs with the flying saucer stickers?" one poster asks. "At least 100 of them all over the Taos area. Anyone know the history of this?"

Some attribute the stickers to bored teenagers, or the Chupacabra. One responder observes that New Mexico's earliest reports of cattle mutilations happened in that same area, just north of Taos. Initially the Highway Department attempted to remove the stickers, but this seemed to make it worse as stickers then began appearing on every Cattle Crossing sign in the region. Another responder answers, simply, "Welcome to Taos!"

*

Dark European: Pardon, Madame… have you not heard?
Englishwoman: We hear very little -- and we understand even less.

*

In the early 1970s, Marshall Applewhite owned and operated a popular deli in Taos. In 1997, Applewhite orchestrated the mass suicide of the Heaven's Gate cult. He and his 39 followers left behind a hilltop mansion in San Diego where they took their own lives, as well as an unfinished 40-acre "earth ship" compound in New Mexico's Manzano Mountains. The Heaven's Gate group lived at the compound for a year in 1995, constructing a border wall made from tires around the site of their planned commune.

"I thought they were out of their minds, even though they were always polite," a local grocer says of the Heaven's Gate members who frequented his store. "They were always talking about God and meeting the spaceship—I guess people didn't think that was weird enough to worry about, since we get lots of UFO stuff around here anyway."

The Heaven's Gate group ran an online business called "Computer Knowmad" out of nearby Mountainair, but eventually abandoned their planned commune and relocated to San Diego in 1996. Applewhite then informed the group, they would—much like the main character in *Close Encounters of the Third Kind*—be hitching a ride on a visiting UFO. Unlike *Close Encounters*, this UFO wasn't going to land at Devils Tower in Wyoming. It was just going to pass by the Earth behind the visiting Hale-Bopp comet. Nevertheless, Applewhite persuasively instructed the Heaven's Gate members that they would be able to board the spaceship via a fatal cocktail of phenobarbital mixed with applesauce and vodka.

In a *New York Times* piece entitled "Heaven's Gate Fit in With New Mexico's Off-beat Style," published shortly after the mass suicide, Carey Goldberg points out that the Manzano area where the Heaven's Gate members temporarily settled also includes "a Hindu retreat; a center for Russian mysticism; at least one survivalist enclave; the Sufi Foundation, a nearby retreat for those who practice Islamic mysticism, and New Age encampments for what some locals call 'burned-out people.' One paramilitary group here has sought to secede from the country." The article suggests that the extraordinarily diverse range of alternative lifestyles that make their home in New Mexico also makes it a haven for cultists and "fringe" types.

"It's very logical that this would happen in New Mexico," suggests Peter White, a professor of folklore at the University of New Mexico. "The history of New Mexico has been this search for spiritual values. I mean, the state is a state that has processions to Chimayó," a New Mexican church that has gained fame for allegedly delivering miracles to worshipful pilgrims. As White explains in the documentary *High Strange New Mexico*, "The spiritual world is right on the surface in New Mexico, so it's natural that the alien world would be right on the surface... belief in aliens and UFOs is a search for spiritual meaning and significance, for spiritual reality."

Given the above, I wonder if my longstanding interest in aliens might be some form of "spiritual reality" I can call my own. I was raised Catholic, but the whole thing just never seemed very plausible to me. Even less so than aliens and flying saucers. My final break with religion came a few years ago when we took my older brother, Louis, off life support. Like the Heaven's Gate followers, he managed overdose on a fatal cocktail—his was OxyContin, Valium, and alcohol. Unlike the Nike-wearing Heaven's Gate folks, this cocktail killed his brain but left me and my parents to finish the job by pulling the plug on his body. When the nurse informed us that Louis had passed, my mother was genuinely disappointed by the absence of any visible signs of his soul departing from the room.

What did she expect? I wondered. A heavenly choir? An ethereal glow?

People believe all sorts of things, I guess. Why not then hitching a ride on a UFO?

*

Ilsa: Can I tell you a story, Rick?

Rick: Has it got a wow finish?

Ilsa: 1 don't know the finish yet.

Rick: Well, go on, tell it. Maybe one will come to you as you go along.

*

Day five in Taos and I've finally made alien contact. Alas it's in the form of the Alien Amber Ale served at the hotel bar where I meet up with some others from the retreat—a young novelist friend from Livorno, Italy; an actor friend from Los Angeles; and a classmate from Oklahoma. I show them all my cerulean blue magnetic bracelet and confess that I am growing a bit skeptical about its healing properties. I then produce the pamphlet which explains that it can heal acne, allergies, asthma, back aches, high blood pressure, bunions, diabetes, carpal tunnel, chronic fatigue, colitis, cramps, earaches, tennis elbow, etc. We collectively consider the bracelet's powers.

"Without pulsed energy there is not life?" my Oklahoma friend reads from the pamphlet in the form of a question. "This is my problem," he observes. "Not enough pulsed energy. That's why I'm so dead inside... *There is not life.*"

"You're always so negative," my Italian friend says. "When was the last time you were happy? I mean, like, genuinely happy?"

"When I was four," my Oklahoma friend replies without irony.

"Oh, come on," my Italian friend says.

"I remember it very clearly."

"Tell us," my Italian friend says.

"Yeah, I want to hear this," my actor friend joins in.

"I was four, playing in a stream. It was beautiful. I was wading into the water, up to my knees, and my father was lifting me up out of the water like this—" my Oklahoma friend throws his arms above his head, lofting an imaginary 4-year-old version of himself into the air with unrestrained joy. "Like this," he repeats, recounting how his father set him back down into the water and then lifted him up again, then down, and up, until his left shoe starting to come off. My Oklahoma friend lowers his arms and describes how his shoe finally got swept away, and how he felt helpless to stop it.

"Why didn't you say something?" I ask.

"I did. I cried, 'Father, my shoe!' But he couldn't hear me. I said, 'My shoe!' And then, just like that, it was gone. And those were my favorite shoes."

"Just like that," my actor friend wipes his beard with a napkin, finishing off a plate of French Fries. "That's a shame," he adds, genuinely sympathetic. "That's really too bad. You couldn't get another?"

"Another shoe? No, I needed a new pair. One's useless without the other."

My Italian friend shakes her head. "Oof."

"You know, that's funny," my actor friend says, snatching a French Fry from the plate of my Oklahoma friend. "How you say that the one shoe was no good without the other. I had a very similar thing happen to me when I was the same age. Maybe a bit older. I had these two toy pistols that I really loved. Just great. Shiny, silver. But the key point is that they were double-holster, matching pistols. I was really so proud of them. It was my birthday party. And at some point, we must have been walking through the woods or something. And I don't know if my friend borrowed them or what, but one of the pistols just disappeared."

"But you still had one?" my Italian friend says. "That's a little better."

"But is it better? Well, I don't know. In some ways it's worse. They were matching pistols with a double-holster, so one is no good without the other."

"You could've put a banana in the holster," my Oklahoma friend adds unhelpfully.

"Well, sure," my actor friend agrees. "But once I realized it was lost, I asked my mom to go back and look for it, but she said no because logically there was just no way. We wouldn't even know where to begin. But it made the whole gift sort of null and void, you know. Having two holsters and the one gun, I mean. It destroyed the value of the gift. My mom just wouldn't do it. And I was just genuinely so upset. It really broke my heart. Years later, she realized that I never forgave her. Before she died it resurfaced. Not the pistol. The whole incident. She still felt guilty about it because I always held it against her. But I don't know that I did, or whether it genuinely affected me."

"I know how you feel," my Italian friend says. "I lost my favorite stuffed animal in the woods."

"Maybe it was the same woods. You don't have my pistol, do you?"

"This was in the mountains in Tuscany," she says. "We were hiking through the woods, with my family, and I had a little stuffed lion. It was Kovu from the *Lion King 2* movie. He was my favorite. Kovu, the bad boy. He had this scar on his cheek and thought he was, like, such hot shit."

"You have a type," I add unhelpfully.

"And Kovu had this girlfriend, Kiara. I don't remember how, but at some point, I lost Kovu along the way. I still had the female but lost the male. And I was so upset. My parents bought me another, but I thought about that little lion all alone in the rain and the mud, by himself, without me, and I just never got over it. I was convinced it had a soul."

Objects with souls. Seems silly at first. But network neuroscience has come to view the human mind as just another kind of complex network, like the World Wide Web, or a power grid. A *Scientific American* article from 2019 called "How Matter Becomes Mind" describes human neural networks as being "reduced to a graph of roughly 300 nodes" which function like "orchestras of neurons that fire together in quite specific patterns." According to this model, "your thoughts, feelings, quirks, flaws and mental strengths are all encoded by the specific organization of the brain as a unified, integrated network. In sum, it is the music your brain plays that makes you *you*."

If this is what makes you *you*—if what shapes your soul comes down to the neural network in your brain—then maybe everything that this network forms a strong attachment to—be it a lost shoe, or pistol, or animal, or friend, or brother—becomes a part of your soul. Our soul.

"I actually lost a stuffed animal too," I join in the conversation. "At an airport when I was like five or six. A teddy bear named Tigger."

"A bear?" my Oklahoma friend interrupts. "Named Tigger?"

"I liked Winnie the Pooh."

"So why didn't you name the bear Pooh?"

"Tigger was my favorite."

"You realize how thoroughly you confused this poor bear."

"Please, continue," my Italian friend says.

"I think your teddy bear ran away. He had an identity crisis."

I concede the point and recount for my friends how I kept setting down my bear on the floor of the airport terminal and then walking away, as if leaving it behind, only to rush back and grab it up again, playing a strange game of abandonment and recovery with the object that I loved most in the world. My mother chastised me at one point, warning that I would lose him for real. And by the time we arrived home, our trip complete, I discovered that she was right, and I had lost him for real. And I wept not only for how I lost my object, but for my complicity in the loss.

"And the worst part was how my brother, who was about nine at the time, kept me taunting me, whispering to me in the dark as I tried to go to sleep that night, saying 'Do you miss your Tigger? He's out there, all alone. Because you left him behind. You lost him.'"

Even now, with Louis dead for ten years, I'm not sure that I have entirely forgiven him for his odd, childish cruelty. I sometimes wonder—knowing full well that I'll never know the answer—if he too was perhaps complicit in the loss.

In Adelaide Bry's *Friendship*, she spends 185 pages describing how to be friends with your parents, your children, employers, ex-lovers, bar pals, fair-weather friends, long- distance friends, your therapist, there's even an entire section dedicated exclusively to "Jewish mothers." But she never once touches on how to be friends with your siblings.

*

Ferrari: We might as well be frank, M'sieur. It will take a miracle to get you out of Casablanca. And the Germans have outlawed miracles.

*

I walk back to my hotel room with my Oklahoman friend, sun setting at 9pm. Dark shades of cerulean blue tread over what's left of a red horizon behind pale mountains. Our conversation from the bar has turned lazy, chasing a thread—something that started with the "freak 8- legged lamb" that we saw at the Governor Bent Museum and turns to H.P. Lovecraft's Dream Realms.

"I've been trying to dream about my brother," I say. Only as the words come out of my mouth do I realize this is true. "I'm not sure why. I've only had three dreams about him in the ten years since he died." The first happened shortly after his death: we say nothing, simply embrace, tightly. Then he walks away. The second, about 5 years later, came while my partner and I were undergoing a series of ultimately unsuccessful attempts at in vitro fertilization. In that dream, my brother points up at three white lights in the sky. "The third one," he says, and again walks away. The last I had just before Taos. In it we are children again, playing an old Atari-style video game. Two 8-bit knights on the TV screen, bouncing on a trampoline over a black chasm. My brother makes it across, but I crash into the castle walls, made of glass, shards rain as enemy-knights storm in, overwhelm us.

"We died," I say in the dream. "Try again?" I ask an empty room.

I return to my hotel room alone, check the skies for signs of aliens and then prepare for sleep, hoping for a dream. Instead, I end up staring at the ceiling for two hours, reflecting on the anxiety attack. I recall how I had just said goodbye to a close friend, a mentor, who was moving to another part of the country. Still reeling from her recent breakup, she slipped away from a farewell party while I was in the restroom. Knowing that this was very likely the last time I would ever see her, I was hurt, and surprised, that she didn't wait to say one last goodbye. I chased her down at the curb and blurted out, "Hey, no goodbye?!"

Clearly the wrong thing to say, and the wrong tone to say it in, she took it as a personal attack, left angrily without a backwards glance. My last image of us reduced to her legs disappearing behind a car door, slammed shut.

Initially I was more confused than upset by the incident. By the next morning, what should've just been a minor glitch in an otherwise beautiful friendship became a cascade of malware windows popping open in my head. A few hours later, on a plane to see my long-distance partner after four months apart, I just couldn't let it go. Staring down at the Wichita Mountains, the cabin walls started to close in. Every mistake I had ever made in my life began storming in through the glass-walls—all those ghosts rattling chains at me.

At the same time, the steady drone of typical in-flight activities—food cart service, announcements, slamming lavatory doors, intermittent glimpses of blue and white lit by sun streaming through portholes—shifted into time-lapse footage, a rainbow blur. I couldn't read, watch, listen to anything, caught in circular thinking. Like William Shatner in that *Twilight Zone* episode where he sees a gremlin on the wing of his plane, everyone around assuming he's having a nervous breakdown. Shatner bangs his fists into his temples, helpless.

Once the plane landed in San Diego, I fell into the arms of my partner, dissolved into a puddle of brokenhearted sobs, and spent the entire car ride home itemizing the issues that our infertility therapist had previously tried to help us resolve.

So here I am in New Mexico, unable to sleep, issues unresolved, magnetic therapy bracelet little help, still waiting for my UFO.

It occurs to me then, finally, only now, that the dreams with my brother are all about trying to say goodbye. I recall now as well, the last time my brother and I ever spoke, about four years before he overdosed. We had a silly argument over what to watch on TV—he was in the middle of *Scarface* and I kept wanting to switch over to the Laker game. He ended up storming out of the room.

"I'm leaving," he snapped.

"See ya," I snapped back, the last words I ever said to him.

The memory reminds me of my latest failed goodbye and how it seemed to trigger my anxiety attack. Saying goodbye to someone you love, especially when you know you'll never see that person again is never easy. But I seem to be especially bad at it. Like I'm grasping for some magical word like "rosebud" in *Citizen Kane*, a final puzzle piece that completes the picture, concludes the story, brings it back to its beginning.

In *Friendship*, Adelaide Bry refers to the *disengagement process* as an essential part of separation, observing, "if you disengage properly, what you are really doing is continuing the friendship process. If you end it in love, you have the option of reactivating the friendship once more, or at least, having good memories."

My favorite writer, David Milch, sums it up best: "It just seems that no matter how much you feel about someone you never really get it squared away. You never really get to understand them the way you wanted." As if the more we feel, the more we want to say, the harder it is to find the language.

Thinking back on it now, I'm struck by how quickly we decided to take my brother off life support once the doctor informed us that he was braindead. We held no hope for a miracle and hated the idea of keeping him alive in a vegetative state. My goodbye to him was wordless. I brushed his sleeping face, gently as I could, afraid to touch him, and left the rest unsaid. If I could go back, all these years later, I'm still not sure what I'd want to say, even if I could find the vocabulary. Maybe that's why my favorite scene in *Close Encounters* has always been when the humans communicate with the aliens through a symphony of music and light. Not quite a heavenly choir and ethereal glow but transcendent in its wordlessness.

The film ends with the main character abandoning his wife and children to fly off with aliens back to their home world. Every time John Williams's dreamy film score melts into a rendition of "When You Wish Upon A Star," I wonder what happens next for the main character. Having escaped from the tedium of daily life, what does he find out there in space? Magical as it might be to abandon this world for the next, does he actually find his heart's desire on some alien world living with extraterrestrials?

Which naturally brings me to the state motto for New Mexico. Known today as "the Land of Enchantment," New Mexico had previously taken to calling itself "the Sunshine State." When Florida nabbed that motto, New Mexico tried on a host of alternatives, including "the Cactus State," "the Spanish State," and "the Land of Opportunity." My favorite of these failed slogans is "the Land of the Heart's Desire."

For all its enchantments, people seem to be drawn to New Mexico in search of a heart's desire, be it healing or high strangeness, artistic inspiration, spiritual elevation, even miracles. Having said that, I recognize that I'm not going to find any aliens here. I will hop aboard their spaceship if they come for me, but I'm not holding my breath. Right now, I just want to fall asleep, maybe have a dream about my brother. One where we can get some things squared away and say a few magic words of goodbye. And because it's a dream, I can hold on to the hope that we might see each other again.

Tom Whalen

Four Micro-Fictions

A Theological Fable

One night a strange exchange occurred: the green man climbed down from his branch in a tree and a priest climbed up to it.

The priest dreamed a child in a yellow dress of moths passed by without noticing the green man asleep on his branch. Then came a mouse with a limp, its left foot once crushed by a trap, and it too ignored the green man adream in the tree of the priest's dream. Next came a crow with too much on its mind to notice anything. Next an ant intent on its own metaphysics.

Hours passed, during which the green man asleep at the foot of the tree dreamed an ant carried a nub of bread to its mound, a crow cawed, a mouse performed figure-8s outside its bolt hole, and a moth alighted on the shoulder of a child in a yellow dress on her way into supper.

———

The Doll in Reality

A doll went to a carnival on a hobby horse. Not really. It only imagined it was at a carnival. In reality the doll wandered the streets of a city in search of other dolls as lonely as it. But instead it came upon a raggedy old poodle who wasn't really a poodle but the night whimpering. Just an old dog, not a doll, thought the doll, and turned into an alley where it saw a bucket that at first it mistook for a child. Inside the bucket was confetti the doll thought was tiny white flags. In the moonlight, the doll covered its naked body with the flags, though what it thought was moonlight was only the glint of a streetlamp in the eye of a mouse in a gutter of the city so desolate only what the doll dreamed was real.

———

From the Diary of a Priest

It's odd that I'm obsessed with the green man I saw sitting on the branch yesterday. Where did he come from? Why did he leer at me, touch my shoulder? Why didn't he answer me when I asked who or what he was, whence his provenance, his address? When he touched me with his forefinger, an electric pain shot through my shoulder and his breath reeked of rotten meat.

Hardly without faith, I feel worn out now by certainty. Up and down my cell I pace, picking up this volume, opening it, reading a few words without any understanding, set it aside, open another, abandon it, ad infinitum.

I am sick, I am mad, I must see him again.

What an obsession corporeality is!

———

Dark Energy

I can't get out of here, I said to the maître d', but she escorted me to the restrooms for pensioners and pulled my pants down. I beg your pardon, she said, then stuck her thumb in my ass. I noticed that the ceiling sagged at the corners. Three nuns wearing cowboy boots entered and said: We can't get out of here either, then left. The maître d' was muttering something I could not understand: *How nicely humanity is enshrouded now.* I think that's what she said. The room smelled of boiled cabbage. Suddenly, as if wafted into the room, a brace of crows …

Impossible to know how far the carrion beetles will drag one, how deep …

Dmitry Borshch

Scoochie

Lee has not slept in four days. Sleeping pills make him nauseous. Breathing regimens, white noise machines, and warm milk prove ineffective. Jumping jacks and pushups leave him panting and trembling, and yet he can not sleep. Lee has suffered bouts of insomnia in the past. His mother had always referred to him as a worrier. He worries about mixing recyclables. He worries about high cholesterol. But most of all, he worries about running out of money, at which point he will be forced to sell his mother's house. Lee quit his teaching job and moved back home when she was diagnosed with grade two brain cancer. She died a month ago.

Lee falls into bed, closes his eyes, and live jazz blares from a neighbor's yard. Outside, people cheer. Horns rattle the window.

Four nights. Four blurry, sleepless nights. Enough to squeeze anybody to paste. And now this music. And Lee was so close! It's as if the universe is determined to compound the turmoil of his life into something concrete. A grand conspiracy against him. But of course that's not it. The neighbors are just assholes. Lee should call the police, but feels it important to maintain a healthy relationship with them. And so he will try to sleep anyway. At least he does not have to be up in the morning.

Drums. Piano. A rogue trumpet. Lee folds the pillow around his head like a taco. The song ends. Applause. A woman shouts *Scoochie*, and the rest of the party cheers and whistles.

"Let's hear a speech, Scoochie!"

Who is Scoochie? A neighbor, apparently, but Lee has never met him. Never heard a single mention from his mother. But the party-goers voices unite: *Scoochie! Scoochie!* and a man answers in articulate Brooklynese. His voice is sober, commanding:

"To be loved by so many," he says, "is a privilege few enjoy. I am a lucky man to have this undying network of support. It's a blessing. Thank you to all of my friends and neighbors for coming. I would be nothing without you. Without community."

The party bursts into wild applause and the band starts again.

What Lee would give for his own undying network of support. Scoochie thanked his neighbors, which implies the neighborhood had been invited. All of them except for Lee. Perhaps nobody was close with his mother, but she'd lived in the neighborhood for forty five years. Been a member of every committee and board imaginable. They all knew her. They knew what she was going through. Too weak to make it to the bathroom by the end. The tumor destroyed her ability to remember names or conversations. Her entire life wiped away. And Lee could do nothing but watch. And this Scoochie could not even take a moment to consider him.

The thought yanks Lee from bed. Naked, he charges to the window and trips on a pair of hiking boots. He falls on his arm and pain shoots up his body. He rolls on the hardwood floor and cradles the injured limb. From outside, glass breaks. The partygoers boo. Lee crawls to the window and pulls himself up.

Every yard is empty. The lights in every house are off. If Lee was deaf, the night would appear just as any other.

But the party noise continues, so loud that it sounds as if it's taking place just below his window, pointed directly at him. He opens the window and sticks his head out to be sure this is not the case. Lee's mother's house is the oldest on the block: a two story colonial built over a hundred years prior floating in a sea of ranches. But they all appear dead in the summer air. No lights. No movement. Nothing save for the noise of the party.

The song ends and the party cheers Scoochie's name. Lee thrusts himself as far out the window as he can and takes another scan of the neighborhood. The party must be happening somewhere on the other side of the house. And yet the noise is right there.

Solid and mocking.

He closes the window and goes back to bed. He needs to sleep. He throws the blanket over him so just his face is exposed. The wall across from him is bare, as is the entire room. His books, clothing, and camping paraphernalia sit in boxes and suitcases on the floor. He sold all of his old furniture and never unpacked after moving into his old bedroom. Packing and leaving his apartment in Atlanta had been easier than expected. No partner to upend or break things off with, no friends to say goodbye to.

Another song ends. "To Scoochie!" a man cheers. Glasses clink, which inspires Lee to go downstairs for water. The kitchen window faces his backyard, and still he hears the party but does not see it. His mother taught him how to make pancakes from scratch in this very kitchen, and on the way back to his room he takes in the entirety of her old home. Walls painted dark red. Farmhouse style trim around the doorways. Antique dolls in a china cabinet. Framed black and white photographs of relatives he cannot name hang on the walls. His height from ages six to fourteen remains penciled in the dining room entranceway. Throw pillows embroidered with Robert Frost poetry arranged on the couch. All of his mother's books shelved and alphabetized. She was responsible for his interest in literature. Showed him Dickinson and Whitman and Thoreau. Encouraged him to move across the country and get his PhD. She was a secretary and had been never granted the luxury of higher education. Even so, Lee felt rotten leaving her alone. He was an only child. His father died in a car accident when he was a baby. All of his grandparents were dead. No aunts or uncles. There was nobody in her life except for him.

He returns to bed and a woman croons over the PA. If only it would end. If only he could fall asleep and for even a few hours, escape his mind. Perhaps he should go over and reason with Scoochie to keep it down. Certainly Scoochie will listen to reason.

Lee puts on a sweatsuit and laces his hiking boots. If Scoochie does not concede, then and only then will Lee call the police.

People outside pound on tables and continue to sing the praise of Scoochie. The entire neighborhood was invited. Everybody except Lee. After all of the *Hellos* and *How-are-yous*. His attempts at good-neighbordom gone unrecognized. In Atlanta, the denizens of his apartment complex were also cold and unwelcoming. He sometimes asked the other faculty in the English department out for drinks, only for them to conjure sudden and forgotten plans. He is positive that his students hated him.

His mind spins, and he no longer hears the party as he crashes down the stairs and flings the door open. He no longer hears the party when he runs out into the front yard. He no longer hears the party at all.

Crickets and the neighbor's sprinklers. A car screeching down the main road two blocks over. But no party. And no noise.

He wanders into the street. Fireflies light around him, what must be hundreds of them glowing on and off like beacons. Lee can't remember the last time he'd seen this many. He always assumed they were near extinction. Is joyed to be wrong.

But the party. There are no cars headed home. No partygoers spilling out into a yard. Nothing. And the noise: absent. No party.

He slaps himself once. Twice. He is not dreaming. The noise of the party is gone. Perhaps it was happening on an adjacent block, and just so happened to end as he exited the house.

He looks up at the sky and spots the constellation Orion. Again, he listens. Silence. Not even crickets. He really must go to bed.

Inside, he pauses at the base of the staircase, grips the cast iron banister, and still hears nothing save the creaking of his old home. Still no party. He returns to his room, slips out of his boots and sweatsuit, and lays in bed.

But the music starts again.

The neighbors are playing a joke on him. They are assholes. Pure assholes. And to think he was going to reason with them. No. The time for reason is over. It may as well be somewhere beyond the horizon, where nobody can touch it. Lee picks up his phone and dials nine-one-one.

A young woman with a southern accent answers. Strange, considering they are on Long Island.

"Nine-One-One what is your emergency?"

"Disturbing the peace," Lee says, the words jumbling in his mouth. Outside, the music swings into uptempo, a cacophony of drum and horn.

"Can you be more specific, sir."

"One of my neighbors is throwing a party," Lee says. "It's so loud." He opens the window and holds the phone out. "Can't you hear it?"

"Do you have the address, sir?" She sounds annoyed.

"No." Which is ridiculous, so he explains, "I can't tell which house it's at." He offers his own address and insists the officer will hear the party once nearby. Another song ends and the partygoers applaud. The operator says that an officer is on the way.

"Is there anything else I can help you with, sir?" she asks. She's the first person Lee has spoken to in days. So many days blending together, feeling the air press down on him.

But Lee tells the operator *No thank you* and hangs up, and the party again cheers the name of Scoochie.

Ten minutes go by. Fifteen. Twenty. Thirty. An hour. The party continues, and no sirens wailing into the night. No squad cars cruising up the block. Nobody knocking on Lee's door. The woman from the band croons and the music presses through the crack around Lee's window, shaking itself into his ear. The party is happening somewhere on the other side of the house, and Lee must find it.

He dashes into his mother's room. Knocks over her antique milk glass lamp. It shatters into powder on the hardwood floor. His stomach twists. Another piece of his mother gone forever. He wants to cry. The music thumps in mockery. He flings the window open, pokes his head out, and there it is, past the sprinklers and the fireflies and the ranch style homes. The next block and ten houses over. The party. The house at which it is happening is built just like his own: colonial, two stories topped by a widow's peak. Lee does not remember the house, which makes no sense. How could he not remember another house exactly like his own and just a block away?

A streetlamp illuminates the house's front yard. Figures shuffle in and out of the back. Lee scrambles to his room to call the police, but remembers previous experience. The police won't help. They are useless. He leaves his phone on the charger. Again dons his sweatsuit and laces up his hiking boots. Marches out the front door.

He marches through the fireflies and down the street. Not a single light other than the streetlamps. All of the houses are dead. Lee stops and glances back towards his mother's, peaking over the one story ranches. Somehow, the party has not grown any louder since he left. He assumed that as he got closer it would, yet the volume remains unchanged. He stops at the mouth of a driveway. A rusty conversion van faces him, its frontend an angry face. Lee turns away from the van, towards the cross street.

The cross street is further now. He swears it is. He counts the houses from his mother's to where he stands. Eighteen. He scrambles another two houses and checks behind him again. Eighteen. He turns back around and again faces the van.

A firefly lands on his arm, glows once, twice, and falls to the ground, dead.

Music. Laughter. Praise of Scoochie. Lee presses on. He doesn't know what else to do, save return to bed. And if he returns to bed he will not sleep.

He trains his eyes on the street corner, and this time reaches it and nothing happens. But why? It makes no sense. He just wants to stretch out on a lawn and fall asleep. He wants to roll in the dewey grass like a child and sail off into unconsciousness. But the party will never allow it. The party must end. He must find Scoochie.

Lee runs. He is about to vomit, and this is how he knows he is not dreaming. He rounds the block and spots the party. He keeps running and it all comes into sharp definition. Men in fedoras and seersucker suits and women in sequined dresses shuffle in and out of the backyard. Heads bop up and down over the horizon of the wooden fence as the band humps along. Now the jazz makes sense. It's one of those Gatsby parties he has seen on the internet. That's what has kept him up all night. Even though it did nothing, he wishes he had called the cops sooner.

He reaches the edge of the lawn and doubles over. Spits bile at the curb. Two women smoking cigarettes glare at him. "Some people should be locked in a cage," a man says. Everybody laughs, but Lee is too nauseous to care. He spits more and wipes his mouth on his sleeve. He scans the face of each passerby and recognizes none. The gate into the backyard is open. There must be hundreds of people, dancing old-timey moves he has seen on TV and in films. Lee glances back and forth across the neighborhood, over the ranches, switching between this house and his mother's. They are painted the same white. Moss covered in the same places. From what Lee can tell, the rooms are even laid out the same: living room to the right of the front door, dining room to the left. On the second floor are two bedrooms facing the street. In every window are figures, silhouetted against the house lights, smoking and dancing and drinking cocktails.

Another man walks by. Lee tugs on his sleeve and asks, "Where is Scoochie?"

But the man smacks Lee's hand away, says, "Who raised you?" and walks on.

Lee's hand stings red, so again he knows that he is not dreaming. He surveys the party once more. Nobody leaves. They shuffle between the house and the front and back yards. There are no cars. Lee asks one after another where Scoochie is, but none answer. How will he ever find Scoochie with all of these people? With all of this noise? The band switches to a slow number and the backyard dancers pair up and sway. The fireflies glow on and off to the rhythm. Lee pushes through the crowd towards the front porch. Like the gate, the front door is wide open. Partygoers filter in and out. Inside, somebody calls Scoochie's name, and Lee charges up the porch after it. Trumpets burst into uptempo from the backyard, Lee crosses over the threshold into the house. The music stops.

The lights are off and the house is empty. The furniture is missing. Everybody is gone. Light shines in from the street and even with the missing furniture, it's the same as walking into his mother's house: the dark red walls, the farmhouse trim around the doorways, the cast iron banister. All the same. Lee checks the front yard. Empty. He slaps himself. Still empty.

His legs wobble. He climbs the creaking stairs to the room that coincides with his mother's. Like the rest of the house, it's empty. It hits him that one day soon his mother's room will be just like this. Lee will be forced to sell or donate most of her things and the rest will be carried off to storage, and then somebody new will move in and redecorate, and it will be as if she never existed. But she existed to Lee. She still does. And one day he too will die, and then the memories of his mother will be wiped away.

Lee opens the window and listens for Scoochie's name. Hears nothing. Now he wants to hear the party and Scoochie's voice, and to meet Scoochie and reason with him to keep the volume down. To have Scoochie drape an arm over his shoulder and offer a beer and introduce him to everybody and to perhaps one day also build his own undying network of support.

Downstairs, somebody stomps. Lee freezes.

"Hello?" he calls. No reply, but the stomping continues. He creeps over to the stairs and repeats, "Hello?" Still nothing save for the stomp stomp stomp. It's coming from the kitchen. "Who's there?"

He left the front door wide open, he realizes.

Stomp. Stomp. Lee grips the cast iron banister and creeps down the rickety old stairs, peaking his head around to see into the kitchen. The street light does not reach. The kitchen is too dark. Stomp. Stomp. He descends the final step and a large figure silhouettes in the kitchen doorframe, its head nearly scraping the top.

"Scoochie?" Lee says. The figure does not reply, because of course it's not Scoochie. Somehow, Lee knows that Scoochie is good, just like he knows that this figure is bad.

The figure stomps into the hallway, and the light from the street reveals an ogrish man in a wifebeater, his skin pocked and pallid, his eyes drooping as if he were melting.

Lee steps back and the man punches the wall. He rips out a chunk of plaster and throws it at Lee. It shatters against the door frame behind him, pelting the back of his head. Lee bolts out the front door and slams it behind him. He is not ready for this. For his life to end. For his memory to be wiped away.

But somewhere in the distance, the music from the party starts again.

The front door of the house remains closed. Lee tenses up, but the door does not open. Carefully, he follows the music through the fireflies and out into the street.

Far, far, far down, opposite of the way he came, now stands a glowing tower, perhaps fifty stories tall. A red neon sign reads *The Scoochie Hotel*. Every light in the building is on, every room illuminated. The street extends much longer than it had before. Like everything else, it doesn't make sense, but Lee hears the party, and without realizing, his feet move one in front of the other through the fireflies and towards the hotel light.

Lee ambles another two houses and something crashes behind him. He turns. The door of the doppelganger house lay splintered across the front steps, and across the lawn the monstrous man charges. Lee runs. He doesn't look back. The man howls after him. Lee translates these howls into direct threats. *Break your legs. Stomp your head.* Lee can't stop. He will be safe at the hotel. It's just a fact, like breathing. The party grows louder. Lee passes house after house. His vision floods with streetlamps, fireflies, hotel rooms, the neon sign. Scoochie. Scoochie can make this all stop. Lee runs and gulps air. His tongue sticks to the roof of his mouth. The horns and drums and piano are like directions, and as if directed, the howling trails further and further behind until it's small and gone.

Lee checks behind him. The street is empty. The monstrous man is gone.

Lee stops. His mother's house and its doppelganger sit far off in the distance. The fireflies whirl around him and a memory glows into his mind: the first time his mother took him camping. She brought Lee to the town campsite. Showed him how to pitch a tent. How to start a fire. The campsite sat on the crest of a hill overlooking a meadow, and Lee and his mother sat by the edge of their fire on the hill and watched over it. There were so many fireflies that night, and Lee realizes that this was the last time he'd seen so many.

He rests against a streetlamp until he's caught his breath. He turns back to the hotel, now just a half dozen houses away. The costumed men and women smoke and drink on the lawn. Music pours from the lobby. A drive circles through the porte-cochere and past the doorway, but there is no parking lot and no cars. Lee checks behind him once more. The monstrous man is truly gone.

But also gone is his mother's house and its doppelganger.

Lee blinks, rubs his eyes. Gone. His eyes well up. His mother. Her memory. Gone.

But this is not true. Lee is still alive, and Lee remembers. It comes ringing into his mind. He remembers. He turns back to the hotel and feels its warm pull. The fireflies make way. Lee does not speak to the people crowded on the lawn, still in their suits and flapper gowns. He weaves through them and the porte-cochere, passing bellboys scurrying into the hotel with luggage.

A pudgy bellboy hauling a suitcase runs into him and the suitcase bursts open and books scatter. "The fuck is wrong with you?" the bellboy says. A breeze tosses the lighter volumes around and the bellboy jumps after them, shoveling the books back into the suitcase. Lee picks a few up.

Their Eyes Were Watching God. The Sun Also Rises. As I Lay Dying. Winesburg, Ohio. Books Lee taught in his last class. His exact copies. Dogeared and post-it noted and spine creased. His name written in the top inside corner of each cover. His head swells like a balloon.

"Watch where you're going," the bellboy says, stuffing *The Age of Innocence* into the suitcase. He zips it shut and on a tag in Lee's handwriting is *Lee Ferguson*. It's one of the suitcases from his room, back at his mother's house.

Two bellboys struggle with his box of camping gear. Others wheel in his suitcases of clothing. The bellboy storms off and a sober, commanding voice shouts in Brooklynese, "Lee Ferguson."

A lanky man in a red pinstriped suit standing by the front door waves to Lee.

This is Scoochie.

Scoochie's hair is bleached blonde, greased and slicked back. He wears a little black moustache. Another bellboy stands at Scoochie's side and Scoochie motions for Lee to come over.

"You look great," Scoochie says. "Doesn't he look great?"

For the first time, Lee checks out his sweatsuit, caked in grass stains and vomit. He checks his reflection in the glass door. His hair is ruffled. He looks like shit.

"We have to get this show on the road. People are waiting. Get all of Mr. Ferguson's stuff in place and get everybody by the stage."

"Right away, sir," the bellboy says.

"Where are they taking my stuff?" Lee asks.

"The invitation said to get here an hour ago."

"I didn't get an invitation."

"All that matters is that you're here."

Lee follows Scoochie into the crowded but cavernous lobby. The air is thick with cigarette smoke. Like his mother's house, the walls are dark red. Marble columns line the center. A massive chandelier hangs from the ceiling, which stretches up to the second floor and a marble balcony overlooks the room. The music comes from deeper within the hotel.

"Scoochie!" a man shouts, and then he notices Lee and shouts, "Lee!" The entire lobby shouts the praise of Lee.

"I wanted you to get here earlier so we could avoid this," Scoochie says.

"Who are you?" Lee asks. "Who are any of these people?"

"Think of them as your undying network of support."

It sounds great, but Lee is tired. So very tired. After all, he has not slept in four days. The people clap and cheer. Men pat him on the back. Women smile and squeeze his elbow. Scoochie pulls Lee by the sleeve and into an empty hallway.

"Have to take the back entrance to get to the stage. You're the main event, you know. The final act."

Of course Lee knows, just like he knew this man was Scoochie and he knew that he would be safe in the hotel and he knew that he would never fall asleep until the party ended.

"Party's got to end eventually," Scoochie says. "Can't until you go on."

"And then I can go to sleep," Lee says, dreamily. Glorious sleep.

"Exactly."

Scoochie opens a metal door labeled *Stage Left*. The door lets out to a curtained area, and past that is the stage. On stage is the band. The one Lee has been following all night.

Horns vibrate his ear. The bass drum thumps his gut. The piano feels like rain. The band finishes and Lee can't see the audience from where he stands, but they cheer. The dozen members of the band stand, take a bow, and file off stage the opposite way of Lee and Scoochie. Bellboys clear the stage and others carry Lee's luggage. They arrange the boxes and suitcases in a semi-circle facing the audience. The pudgy bellboy from earlier and another wheel an upholstered, king sized bed into the semi-circle. The sheets, the comforter, the pillow are all dark red, like Lee's mother's house. Again, he wants to sob. He misses her so much. He misses her house. And they're both gone. He wants to fall into the bed and finally drift away. He just wants to sleep. Temporary escape.

But Scoochie said that he is the grand finale.

"What does it mean?" Lee asks.

Scoochie pulls a rope and a banner unfurls from the rafters. It says, *We Love You, Lee!*

The cheers grow louder. From the side opposite Lee, an old woman in a big white dress hobbles on stage to the bed.

She is Lee's mother.

How can this be? She is dead. Lee watched it happen. He watched her die. He watched her suffer. She pleaded for death. Lee held her hand as she closed her eyes and went to sleep for the last time.

"What is this?" Lee yells. It can't be real. It's an awful, disgusting joke. "What the fuck is this?"

But Scoochie puts his hand on Lee's shoulder and says, "We love you," and suddenly like everything else, Lee knows that it's not a joke. His mother pulls the blanket and waves him over. He remembers her sick. He remembers her withering in bed. And he remembers her dead. She pats the bed and the audience goes atomic. From somewhere in the audience a chant begins: *Lee. Lee. Lee. Lee.* Their cheers turn primal. Blood-curdling. Their voices break. They stomp and pound their seats. Lee's mother pats the bed again and mouths *bedtime* and Lee wants to tip over. It's been four days since he last slept. Scoochie pushes Lee forward and he keeps going, pulled towards the magnetism of the bed. He passes the curtain and steps out into the light of the stage. His mother. He wants to hold her and cry. The audience. All of these people. They will never forget him or his mother. He and his mother are the grand finale. They will be remembered, and they are loved. The shrieks intensify, but even with the light and screams, Lee knows that his mother will tuck him into bed and kiss him on the forehead and he will finally sleep.

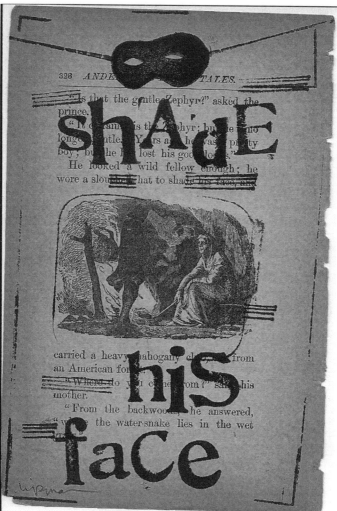

Joel Lipman

David Luntz

The Secret History of Fritz Lang*

I.   Death in Venice (Hollywood), August 2, 1976

Fritz Lang is dying in Los Angeles. But outside his window, he hears from all of forty-six years before, Mimi, the African elephant, screaming. Her hooves pound down the *Unter den Linden*, seeking acacia trees to rub her sores against, the savannah's long cool grass to shelter in. Further down, Roger, the albino rhino, bellows in the Brandenburg Fountain, churning water into frothy rainbows. Morris, the parrot, now cageless, sings giddy canticles, cartwheeling through Roger's rainbows. His eyes blaze brighter than sunlight bouncing off tips of birring blades.

The shirtless zookeeper, Hans, woken up too early, is hurling abuse at the escaped creatures, cracking his *sjambok*. His thin mustache is combed as finely as sand in a miniature Japanese garden. Frau Lisbet, his wife, follows gingerly behind him barefoot, her nightgown billowing like a silk parachute, a dandelion swept off on an abrupt breeze. Frau Lisbet has stepped in Brie cheese on her flight out the house, and, as she floats by Fritz Lang, he knows what angel feet taste like.

A lorry full of Brown Shirts arrives. A firetruck of firemen in black lederhosen set up barricades behind them. Fritz hears a shot, like a starter pistol. It's Hans's whip striking Morris. The whip has a steel-barbed tip. A flurry of gold, violet and black feathers settle over Fritz like a peacock gown. Morris shrieks and flies off into the early morning summer light.

Fritz is hiding behind some bushes, much as he does behind his camera. He wishes he'd brought it along. The day before he had stolen the keys to the Zoo and early this morning, he'd let the animals out as a lark, as a midlife crisis prank. As a chance to turn a zoo into a fleeting or fleeing circus. To make something horribly cruel a little less cruel. To have a good laugh, too. Or, so he thought. Now he sees it was his first act of sabotage against everything he detested.

He's not sure how he never saw it before. Perhaps, the distraction of making movies blinded him. Or, all the awards he won. But he dies happy in this final knowledge. The crowning achievement of his life.

The last thing he hears is Morris singing the "Queen of the Night" and the bleeding colors of the setting sun pitter-pattering like soft rain on broad coconut leaves.

II.　　Berlin Zeitgeist, Afternoon Edition, July 27, 1930
　　　　(Reprinted in *The Times of London, Associated Press,* and
　　　　The New York Herald Tribune)

Early this morning, the gates to the animals in the Berlin Zoo were mysteriously unlocked. Most of the animals escaped. They wreaked havoc on the Unter den Linden and other nearby thoroughfares. Damage to private and public property is expected to exceed 1,000,000 Reichsmarks. Foul play is suspected. A reward of 10,000 Reichsmarks has been established for any information leading to the person or persons responsible for this criminal mischief.

The fortuitous arrival of a marching band of Hitlerjugend and local firemen coming off their night shift, however, resulted in the quick and efficient capture of the animals. All of them are now safe back in their cages and the Zoo is expected to reopen to the public tomorrow.

Only a much beloved Fijian parrot named "Morris" remains at large. Morris is believed to be 80 years old and sings popular opera arias in German, French, English, Italian and Russian. Sightings of him have been reported in Nuremberg and Munich.

Contacted by telephone, Professor Gerhardt Mauser, Director of the Zoological faculty at the University of Heidelberg and a world authority on Psittaciformes, stated, "Parrots never forget where they come from. Morris is trying to fly home. I wish him the best of luck in this endeavor."

III.   Excerpt from Fritz Lang's Diary, January 7, 1965, Los Angeles

...dreamt again of that damn bird. *Maurice.* Christ, I hope he made it. Damn long way, Berlin to Fiji. But maybe not impossible. If the Soviets can put a man in space, why not?

Sometimes, I sense some music in me but I cannot hear it. It's like some other life is living through me and I wander through mine in night and fog, so much darkness concealing the way to inner sight or that other life...*ach*, foolish ramblings from an old man, but I wonder if *maybe* there is a secret history to my life...and what I was really put here to do was to free a bird who sang opera and, in this way, put Mozart in the jungle...

* Friedrich Christian Anton "Fritz" Lang (December 5, 1890 – August 2, 1976) was an Austrian-German-American film director. He fled Nazi Germany in 1933, first to Paris and then Los Angeles. He directed many cinematic classics like *Metropolis*, *The Testament of Dr. Mabuse*, *Scarlet Street* and *The Big Heat.*

Quentin Bailey & Harold Jaffe
Dream Discourse

WEEP

I know a soul who weeps over roadkill but turns his back at a CEO's death.
The globe is swaying, about to slip off its axis.
Like the revolution of the just, weeping has lost all leverage.
Every wall erected to keep creatures out is a wailing wall.
My charge is revival.
Transforming torment into a principle of conquest.

I propose a collective Weep-In.
Global.
Not excluding Black Africa and Bangladesh and East Timor.
Not excluding the aged whom the electronic "revolution" has left behind.

Weeping animals along with plants and stones traverse the benighted globe.
Commencing in the west, swaying south, east, north.
Even as I walk hand-in-hand / hand-in-paw, weeping, I stand sad-eyed by the gravest, the worst-suffering.

I pass my hand over their heads.

They are impressive in their weeping.

Tormented, restless, they weep until bloody, fruitless wars are over.

Climate change acknowledged, addressed.

Dehumanizing post-capitalism hacked, disempowered.

The invisible colored poor made visible.

The twisted made sound.

Enslaving technology disappeared.

The preceding was based on a dream I had after rereading portions of Whitman's 1855 edition of *Leaves of Grass*.

Dream: *The Prelude*

Wordsworth dreams of an Arab riding across the desert on a camel. He is carrying two books: one is a stone and the other a shell. The stone, to the dreaming Wordsworth, is a copy of Euclid's *Elements*, telling of a world undisturbed by the pressures of space or time. The shell, which he holds to his ear at the bidding of the Arab, foretells great disturbances in this world:

> Destruction to the children of the earth
> By deluge, now at hand.

The Arab is on his way to bury both books, hoping to save them from the 'waters of the deep' that threaten to swamp the arid plains where he and Wordsworth find themselves.

The dream is not really Wordsworth's. In earlier versions of *The Prelude* it is ascribed to a friend. Coleridge has been mentioned as one possibility, though that would seem cumbersome in a poem originally written for him. Michel Beaupuy, the French revolutionary who befriended the young poet, is a more credible candidate. In neither case was the dream really theirs. It is a version of one Descartes had in November 1619. That dream involved two books—a dictionary or encyclopaedia and an anthology of poetry—and led Descartes to the philosophy that inaugurated the Enlightenment.

In Wordsworth's non-dream, which he experiences while sleeping in a cave, the Arab shifts in and out of the character of Don Quixote:

> He, to my fancy, had become the knight
>
> Whose tale Cervantes tells; yet not the knight,
>
> But was an Arab of the desert too;
>
> Of these was neither, and was both at once.

Descartes and Cervantes: the stone and the shell, the philosophical truths of geometry and the power of poetry 'to exhilarate the spirit' by retelling dreams. It is a dichotomy that goes back at least as far as Plato.

The desert dweller abandons Wordsworth to the onrushing waters, yet still earns his admiration. There are enough other people in the world, the poet reasons, to take care of the vulnerable. A semi-Quixote determined to save the products of human ingenuity rather than the lives of real people is only a maniac in a dream. He is Descartes and Cervantes, scientist and storyteller, and both or neither at once.

FIRE

A survivor of the vast Australian fires writes:

"We felt a new and special way of being afraid. There was the fear of the things itself—the enormous wall of flame and its greed, fire chomping through entire towns down to the water's edge. Then there was the other fear. Flashes of a deeper dread—an apprehension of an ending."

Is the idea here that nature itself is willfully retaliating?

Someone put it this way:
"The billionfold vegetable dead who surround us

have more wisdom, prescience and mute compassion

than those humans allegedly alive gazing at their smartphones while the world perishes."

Wasn't that "someone" yourself?
*You said it in your volume **Revolutionary Brain**.*

Death Café.

*All right, **Death Café**?*
Do you mean to anthropomorphize nature?

No. Responding willfully, even with consciousness, is not
strictly the province of humans.
You didn't hear of the ancient script in Icelandic found on the remnants of a
glacier in the Arctic after a portion the size of Texas broke off?
it said: **Humankind Beware!**

Icelandic?

Maybe it was in the Antarctic and the script was in Tamil.

You're not making this up, are you?

No, I'm not making it up.

*But do I believe that nature—what's left of it—is in a sense willfully retaliating
against human depredation?*
Irrespective of those "scripts" that you refer to, I would say Yes, I do.
So where does that leave us?

If us represents the many millions of humans born into technology,
so to speak, it leaves us in an unimaginable, but not entirely undesirable space.
Many of those young humans informed by "hi-technology" are convinced
they will live forever, perhaps immaterially on an electronic "platform."

Meanwhile they will gladly share our devastated freeways with AI, refined humanoids with very white teeth.

You know how hard it is for Americans to resist very white teeth.

You've heard of the buccal corridor, right?

No. I don't know it.

Google it.

There is also the further possibility of hitching a ride to outer space with one of our billionaires.

They do have their sights set on colonizing outer space, don't they?

And the more billionaires shoot into space the lower the price will be to join in the new colonization.

The new old colonization.

Yes, but not all young folk are blind to biological nature.

Consider Greta and her army of teens and adolescents.

You don't expect that Greta and her teen army will continue to make noise on behalf of humankind as we know it?

Greta does not have very white teeth.

When she smiles, which is rare--what is there to smile about?
When Greta smiles her rare smile she does not display her teeth.

Which signifies what?

That Greta will not be an actor in the larger drama.

Truly?
That is very sad to hear.
I'm wondering: are those humanoid billionaires colonizing outer space artificially constructed?

Depends what you mean by artificial.
If you mean not biologically conceived in the way we generally define those words,
The answer would be Yes.
In the meantime "artificial" is rapidly replacing the traditional "real."

None of this is good news.

You want good news, check out your smartphone.

I think I'll have a bath with Epsom salts and go to sleep.

Watch out for your dreams.

What do you mean?
Are you suggesting that some of this bad shit has infected my dreams?

You tell me.
Write them down if you need to.
When we meet again next week tell me what you've been dreaming.

Meet again here?

It is a congenial spot, no?

Yes.
Will the poppies be as good?

I'm glad you've enjoyed yourself.
Both De Quincey and Coleridge insisted that opium was a truth-teller.
Mad Artaud did as well. Cocteau. Graham Greene, too.
It is a long list.
Why is it that so few female writers have written about opium?

Now that is a pertinent question, and I think the response will surprise you.
Let's resume with that when we meet next week.

Dream: *Confessions of an English Opium-Eater*

Thomas De Quincey's dreams expand across time and space, obeying no rational limits, and knowing no restraint. They are comparable to the dramatic effects of storm clouds in the mountains. He turns to Wordsworth's *Excursion* to describe these experiences, quoting from the Solitary's sudden vision of the 'New Jerusalem' to give a sense of the constant swelling, the ebb and flow, of drug-shaped dreams and utopian fantasies:

> The appearance, instantaneously disclosed,
> Was of a mighty city—boldly say
> A wilderness of building, sinking far
> And self-withdrawn into a wondrous depth,
> Far sinking into splendour—without end!
> Fabric it seem'd of diamond, and of gold,
> With alabaster domes, and silver spires,
> And blazing terrace upon terrace, high
> Uplifted …

A sudden break in the mist has granted the Solitary, a disappointed revolutionary, this view of a new world, 'the revealed abode of spirits in beatitude'. It is something, Wordsworth writes, the Hebrew Prophets might have beheld.

De Quincey gives another example to illustrate the ways in which lived experiences swell almost beyond recognition in dreams: Piranesi's *Carceri d'Invenzione*. This time he turns to Coleridge, a fellow opium-eater, and recounts his description of an artist trapped within his imaginings:

> Creeping along the sides of the walls, you perceived a stair-case; and upon it, groping his way upwards, was Piranesi himself: follow the stairs a little further, and you perceive it come to a sudden abrupt termination, without any balustrade, and allowing no step onwards to him who had reached the extremity, except into the depths below. Whatever is to become of poor Piranesi, you suppose, at least, that his labours must in some way terminate here. But raise your eyes, and behold a second flight of stairs still higher: on which again Piranesi is perceived, but this time standing on the very brink of the abyss. Again elevate your eye, and a still more aerial flight of stairs is beheld: and again is poor Piranesi busy on his aspiring labours: and so on, until the unfinished stairs and Piranesi both are lost in the upper gloom of the hall.

In these imaginary prisons, human subjects are threatened by technological power and dwarfed by the sheer scale of the architecture. Plate III is one such example: the inmates, destined to wander the halls and staircases forever, are eternally lost. Space, in these drawings, expands infinitely, offering new perspectives within which the individual can be confined. In plate II of the 1760 series even the pediment of an external church becomes enclosed within the architectural space of the prison.

De Quincey recounts his own dream, without the mediation of Wordsworth or Coleridge. It is of the Malay, his 'fearful enemy', who transports him to Asia each night. There he is confronted with the 'antiquity of Asiatic things' and the feeling that this is 'the part of the earth most swarming with human life'. He shudders at the 'mystic sublimity of *castes* that have flowed apart, and refused to mix, through such immemorial tracts of time'. It makes him feel that he is the idol, the priest, the sacrifice, the buried outlaw, and the discarded evildoer 'confounded with all unutterable slimy things, amongst reeds and Nilotic mud.'

For De Quincey, our dreams are acts of expansion, but the human subject is not liberated by this work of the imagination: Piranesi is trapped within the vast prisons of his invention; the Solitary's vision of towers in the clouds is haunted by its almost parodic proximity to castles in the sky; and the Malay embodies the faces, 'imploring, wrathful, despairing', that tyrannize over our nightmares. Wordsworth's episode is controlled by contradictory verbal images, with depths raised to the level of wonder, and buildings creating a wilderness; Piranesi's vision relies on the multiple perspectives of baroque mechanics; and De Quincey's on tinctures of opium. But all understand individual experience as threatened by imaginative overreach.

A Malay, De Quincey tells us earlier in the *Confessions*, showed up at his Lake District house one day. They could not communicate but he allowed him to rest for a bit. As his guest departed, De Quincey gave him three pieces of opium, assuming his unknown visitor would know what it was. He bolts the opium down immediately, much to his host's consternation. 'The quantity was enough to kill three dragoons and their horses.' Was the Malay looking to lighten the loneliness of his wanderings, seeking in dreams the compassion he could not find on his travels? Was he hungry?

Wordsworth's Solitary was part of a rescue mission for an old man who had gone missing with a mountain storm brewing. The team search into the evening, but return to their homes when the storm grows too strong. They find the old man the next day, disoriented but alive. As he follows the shepherds carrying the man down the mountain, the Solitary is granted his vision of the 'New Jerusalem' and 'utterly' forgets the Old Man, who dies three weeks later.

De Quincey was more fortunate. There were no reports of a dead Malay. 'I must have done him the service I designed, by giving him one night of respite from the pains of wandering'.

INFECT DREAM

It was thought—though with trepidation—
that the last uncolonized space in a chronically intrusive world
was dream.

Of course, sleep and dream have long been intruded on by medication,
but now, inevitably, the dollar has found ways to "weaponize" our
dreams so that the victimized sleeper dreams of Coors Beer, Nike, and the
forever brand new Apple iPhone.

The concept is called "dream incubation," techniques employed while
the targeted human is awake to induce that person to dream about the advertised
product while asleep.

Pleasant dreams, Darling!

Contributors

Benjamin Abtan is the child of Moroccan immigrants to France, an immigrant to the US himself, he has dedicated his life to advancing social justice. With over 20 years of involvement, he built an international network of community-led antiracist organizations and developed a "Dialogue of Memories" with genocide survivors in Rwanda. His non-fiction work has been featured in *The Guardian, Le Monde, La Repubblica, El Pais, Die Zeit, Le Soir, The Sunday Times, Die Welt, Corriere della Sera,* and elsewhere.

Quinn Adikes' work has appeared in *Five Points, Epiphany, The Southampton Review,* and other journals. He is the recipient of the Joseph Kelly prize for writing and has been nominated for a Pushcart Prize. He lives in Brooklyn and has an MFA from Stony Brook Southampton. You can find out more about him at Quinnadikes.me

Quentin Bailey is an Associate Professor in the Department of English and Comparative Literature at San Diego State University. His work focuses on the political and ethical commitments of Romantic-era writing, with a particular emphasis on the works of William Wordsworth and William Hazlitt. His first book, *Wordsworth's Vagrants*, was published by Ashgate in 2011 and he is currently at work on studies of the political contexts of Hazlitt's art criticism and the ethical implications of Wordsworth's poems. His work has appeared in *The Wordsworth Circle, Romanticism, European Romantic Review, Eighteenth-Century Literature, Charles Lamb Bulletin, Nineteenth-Century Studies, Comparative Literature,* and *Twentieth-Century Literature.*

R. Bennett was the founding editor of *The Southern Anthology*. His work has been widely published in venues including *Brooklyn Review, Columbia Journal, Indiana Review, New World Writing, Bombay Review* (INDIA), *Galway Review* (IRELAND), and *Paris-Transcontinental - Sorbonne* (FRANCE). His novel, *The Final Yen*, was recently released by Sunbury Press, and his fiction collection, *A Taste Of Heaven*, is upcoming from Tailwinds Press.

Dmitry Borshch was born in Dnipropetrovsk, studied in Moscow, today lives in New York. His works have been exhibited at Russian American Cultural Center (New York), HIAS (New York), Consulate General of the Russian Federation (New York), Lydia Schukina Institute of Psychology (Moscow), Contemporary Art Centers (Voronezh, Almaty), Museums of Contemporary Art (Poltava, Lviv).

Robert Boucheron is an architect in Charlottesville, Virginia. His short stories and essays appear in *Bellingham Review, Christian Science Monitor, Fiction International, Louisville Review, New Haven Review,* and *Saturday Evening Post*. He is the editor of *Rivanna Review*. His blog is at robertboucheron.com

Elizabeth Brus' debut fiction was published in *The Normal School* in 2022. She has a B.A. in English and Creative Writing from Columbia University, and a M.Sc. in Creative Writing from The University of Edinburgh. She lived in Lesotho from 2005-2007.

Douglas Cole has published six collections of poetry and the novel, *The White Field*, winner of the American Fiction Award. His work has appeared in several anthologies as well as journals such as *The Chicago Quarterly Review, Poetry International, The Galway Review, Bitter Oleander, Chiron, Louisiana Literature, Slipstream*, as well Spanish translations of work in *La Cabra Montes*.

Robert James Cross is a Pushcart Prize-nominated writer. He has an MFA in Fiction from San Diego State University. His writing has been published in previous issues of *Fiction International* ("The Body" & "Algorithm"). Cross lives in San Diego but is originally from Hollywood, CA. He believes the unconventional is the sine qua non of understanding.

Michelle DeLong is an MFA candidate from Wyoming whose work has appeared or is forthcoming in The New York Times and Nowhere Magazine.

Mark DiFruscio is currently a PhD candidate in English at Oklahoma State University. Her previously published work has appeared in *Fiction International, The Laurel Review,* and *Puerto del Sol*, and his story "The Alien Dialogues" was selected as one of the winners of the 2020 AWP Intro Journals Project.

Arthur M. Doweyko is a scientist who has authored 140+ scientific publications, invented novel 3D drug design software, and shares the 2008 Thomas Alva Edison Patent Award for the discovery of Sprycel, a new anti-cancer drug. He writes and illustrates science fiction, fantasy and horror, and has maintained a life-long love of art.

Nancy J. Fagan's recent work is forthcoming or can be read in *The Garfield Lake Review, Bright Flash Literary Review, The Headlight Review, Breath & Shadow, You and Me Medical Magazine,* and *Abilities, Canada,* among others. She is a registered nurse, holds a BA in English from Mount Holyoke College and and received an MFA in Writing from the Vermont College of Fine Arts. She lives in western Massachusetts with her husband and two ridiculous cats. Please visit nancyjfagan.com for more information.

Susan A. H. Grace is a California writer with work published in *Orca Literary Journal, Fiction International, Autre Magazine,* and elsewhere. She is a Pushcart Prize nominee and received her MFA from San Diego State University in 2018.

Brandon Hansen is a Truman Capote Scholar at the University of Montana's MFA program. His work has appeared or is forthcoming in *Puerto Del Sol, The Baltimore Review, LIT Magazine*, and elsewhere.

Sara Jacobson is based out of New York City and teaches English Composition at The City College of New York.

Harold Jaffe is the author of 30-plus books of fiction, docufiction, and essays, most recently *Sacrifice*; *Brando Bleeds*; *Strange Fruit and other Plays*; *BRUT: Writings on Art & Artists*, and *Performances for the End of Time*. Jaffe is editor-in-chief of *Fiction International*.

Marc Levy's work has appeared in *New Millennium Writings, Stone Canoe, Counter Punch, The Comstock Review, The Bosphorus Review of Books, Stand* and elsewhere. It is forthcoming in *Calliope* and *Queen's Quarterly*. He won the 2016 Syracuse University Institute for Veterans and Military Families Writing Prize. His website is MedicintheGreenTime.com

Joel Lipman's collection of 40 visual poems, *from The Origins of Poetry*, is a 2022 hardbound publication from Redfoxpress. Emeritus Professor of English at the University of Toledo, he lives in Michigan and Maine.

Nathan Alling Long's work has won international competitions and appears on NPR and in various journals, including *Tin House, Story Quarterly, Witness,* and *The Sun. The Origin of Doubt*, a collection of fifty stories, was a 2019 Lambda finalist.

David Luntz has work in *Best Small Fictions* (2021), *Pithead Chapel, Vestal Review, trampset, X-R-A-Y Lit,* and other print and online journals. Twitter: twitter.com/luntz_david

Stephen-Paul Martin is a widely published writer of fiction, non-fiction, and poetry.

James McNally served as a medic in the United States Air Force Medical Service. He went on to a forty-five-year career in the health care field. He has traveled extensively in the United States and Europe and this is his first published work of fiction.

Elaine Monaghan is a much-published former foreign correspondent who grew up in a tiny village in Scotland and teaches journalism at Indiana University.

Toby Olson's most recent book, *Journeys on a Dime: Selected Stories*, appeared from Grand Iota press a few months ago. His recent poetry selection, *Death Sentences*, was published by Shearsman. Currently, it's poetry that keeps him busy.

Robert L. Penick's poetry and prose has appeared in over 100 different literary journals, including *The Hudson Review, North American Review,* and *Plainsongs*. His latest publication is *Exit, Stage Left*, from Slipstream Press, and more of his work can be found at theartofmercy.net

Adam Peterson is the author of the flash fiction collections *My Untimely Death*, *The Flasher*, and *[SPOILER ALERT]* (with Laura Eve Engel). His fiction has appeared in *Epoch, The Kenyon Review, The Southern Review,* and elsewhere.

AE Reiff has published in *Emanations, Sidebrow, Manneqin Haus, Ygdrasil, Lifted Brow, Café Irreal, Gobbet* and *Frigg*.

William Repass lives in Pittsburgh, Pennsylvania. His poetry and prose have appeared in *Word For / Word, Denver Quarterly, Hotel Amerika, Bending Genres, Cabildo Quarterly,* and elsewhere. His critical writing can be found at *Full Stop* and *Slant Magazine*.

J. Condra Smith is a queer writer with roots in Mexico and the U.S. He recently earned his MFA from The University of Maryland, where he taught creative writing. This is his first publication.

Suzana Stojanović, an artist and writer, studied literature at the Faculty of Philosophy of the University of Niš in Serbia. She is the author of the book *The structure and meaning of the border stories of Ilija Vukićević* and many literary, artistic, and philosophical texts, short stories, satires, essays, and poems. Website: suzanastojanovic.com

Nick Sweeney's books include a haunted jaunt around Poland in *Laikonik Express* (Unthank Books, 2011), a wander in the wrong part of Silesia in *The Exploding Elephant* (Bards and Sages, 2018), a look at genocide survivors in1960s *Nice in A Blue Coast Mystery, Almost Solved* (Histria Books, 2020). As a photographer, Sweeney takes too many photos, hoping some will work. They have appeared in *Riding Light, Every Pigeon* and *Thirty West*.

Tom Whalen's books include *The President in Her Towers*, *Elongated Figures*, *Winter Coat*, *The Straw That Broke*, *Dolls*, and most recently his second selection and translation of short prose by Robert Walser, *Little Snow Landscape* (NYRB Classics).

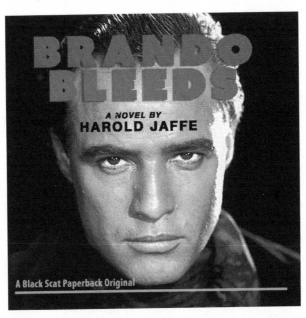

A "docufictional" version of the life of renegade cultural icon Marlon Brando. Harold Jaffe seamlessly weds biographical fact and fiction, breathing new life into Brando as shaman/showman, an anti-Hollywood "movie star" whose radical politics forced him to confront the inevitable contradiction between rebel/activist and capitalist avatar. Drawn from biographical sources and Brando's films, the author unveils Brando as a unique artist who both witnesses and introjects the world in pain.

BRANDO BLEEDS by Harold Jaffe. Paperback; 181 pp., $14.95

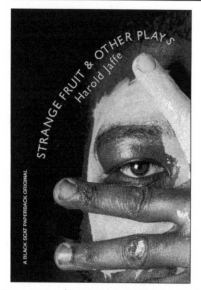

Made in the USA
Columbia, SC
30 October 2022

70065352R00140